HIS SWEET TORMENT

A BAD BOY BILLIONAIRE ROMANCE

MICHELLE LOVE

HOT AND STEAMY ROMANCE

CONTENTS

About the Author	v
Sign Up to Receive Free Books	vii
Blurb	1
1. Chapter one	3
2. Chapter two	15
3. Chapter three	25
4. Chapter four	33
5. Chapter five	44
6. Chapter six	54
7. Chapter seven	61
8. Chapter eight	72
9. Chapter nine	74
10. Chapter ten	84
11. Chapter eleven	97
12. Chapter twelve	104
13. Chapter thirteen	108
14. Chapter fourteen	120
15. Chapter fifteen	127
16. Chapter sixteen	134
17. Chapter seventeen	139
18. Chapter eighteen	145
Sign Up to Receive Free Books	149
Preview of The Midnight Club	150
Dusk - Midnight Club Part 1	152
Other Books By This Author	219
About the Author	221
Copyright	223

Made in "The United States" by:

Michelle Love

© Copyright 2020 – Michelle Love

ISBN: 978-1-64808-078-4

ALL RIGHTS RESERVED. No part of this publication may be reproduced or transmitted in any form whatsoever, electronic, or mechanical, including photocopying, recording, or by any informational storage or retrieval system without express written, dated and signed permission from the author

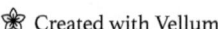 Created with Vellum

ABOUT THE AUTHOR

Mrs. Love writes about smart, sexy women and the hot alpha billionaires who love them. She has found her own happily ever after with her dream husband and adorable 6 and 2 year old kids.
Currently, Michelle is hard at work on the next book in the series, and trying to stay off the Internet.
"Thank you for supporting an indie author. Anything you can do, whether it be writing a review, or even simply telling a fellow reader that you enjoyed this. Thanks

Facebook
facebook.com/HotAndSteamyRomance

Instagram
instagram.com/michellesromance

SIGN UP TO RECEIVE FREE BOOKS

Sign Up to Receive Free E-Books and Audiobook Codes.

Would you like to read **The Unexpected Nanny, Dirty Little Virgin** and **other romance books** for **free**?

You can sign up to receive these free e-books and audiobooks by typing this link into your browser:

https://www.steamyromance.info/free-books-and-audiobooks-hot-and-steamy/

Or this one:

https://www.steamyromance.info/the-unexpected-nanny-free/

BLURB

Three days before newly graduated FBI agent Padme Kaur is due to start her new assignment –protecting an Italian dignitary —she attends the restaurant opening of a good friend and sees him. He's gorgeous, mysterious—and judging by his appalling American accent— hiding his true identity.
But Padme has never met such a sensual, incredible man and throws all caution to the wind. For the next three days, her enigmatic lover introduces her to a world of erotic pleasure the likes of which Padme has never dreamed of. Saying goodbye to him on Sunday night, Padme feels bereft, knowing she will never forget him.
So, when she walks into her Seattle field office Monday morning, the last person she is expecting to see is her lover. Their unexpected reunion is further complicated when Padme learns that her weekend fling is her first assignment—and a high-profile one at that.
Billionaire industrialist Enver Toscano is in trouble. Big trouble. His business partner has just been murdered and now Enver has been dragged into the aftermath of his shady deals, with a death

threat hanging over him. His only way out is to testify in court against the men threatening him, and now the FBI are tasked with protecting him—and Padme and her partner Dale have been chosen to guard him.

CHAPTER ONE

Harpa malhotra shrieked with joy as she threw her arms around padme. "you came! Here i thought you'd be too locked into your first assignment to show up."

Padme kaur hugged her friend. "miss your restaurant opening? Never, baby, never."

Harpa grinned at her. "you're such a good friend. Now, let's go get really drunk and check out all the handsome boys i hired as wait staff."

Padme laughed. "what will mikah say?" Mikah ray was harpa's long-time boyfriend, a sweet, serene african-american whom padme adored. Harpa grinned.

"oh, i hired some pretty girls too. I'm not stupid." She looked padme up and down. "speaking of which, you look gorgeous."

Padme grinned shyly. She was wearing a dark gold sheath dress which clung to her curvy body in all the right places and dipped low at the back, revealing a silky expanse of dusky skin. Her chestnut brown hair, thick and wavy, hung to the middle of her back. She'd made up her face with only the barest minimum of makeup, preferring the natural look, but there was a hint of pink blush on her cheeks and a rosy tint to her lips. Padme wasn't ignorant of her natural beauty; it was that just it didn't mean anything significant to her. She would rather be complimented on her intellect or her sense of humor. At quantico, she'd had to fight hard to shake off the mantle of beauty over brains—finishing at the top of the class had helped that. Her usual uniform of jeans and t-shirt had been forgone tonight though, and padme had enjoy getting dressed up for this party,

Harpa, no slouch in the looks department herself, grinned at her friend, but then glared at her in mock-disapproval. "you'd better not stand too close to cosima—way too much beauty. You'll both break all the men present."

She dragged padme, laughing, into the main room of harpa's new seattle-based restaurant, bedi. Bedi had been harpa's pseudonym when she had switched careers from fashion styling to her passion, cooking, a few years ago, and now harpa was one of the most sought-after chefs in the world. Padme had met harpa soon after harpa had suffered through a traumatic time with her lovely older sister, cosima. Cosima had been shot and nearly killed by her own fbi protector, jack hampton, and it had been that shocking attempted murder that had inspired padme to go into training at quantico.

Padme, at twenty-eight, knew all about betrayal. Her birth mother had given her up, and she had spent years in the foster care system, alone and vulnerable. When she was thirteen, she was assaulted by one of her guardians, a kind-faced man called robert. Robert had threatened to kill padme if she ever told anyone about the assault, and she had never forgotten the feeling of having her trust wrenched away from her.

Despite her difficult start to life, padme was persistent. She had worked three jobs to pay for college and had been headhunted by a man called henry jones to enter the program at quantico. Padme had been top of her class, and now she was three days away from her first assignment. She was nervous but excited about the job, and right now she just wanted to kick back and relax on this last friday before her new start.

Harpa returned with some drinks, including a violently bright cocktail that looked lethal. Padme chuckled at the mischievous expression on harpa's face. The cocktail was potent, but delicious, and padme felt any tension about her upcoming assignment slide away.

She spotted cosima and went to greet her. Cosima glowed with health and pregnancy— her fifth, harpa had told padme with an astonished shake of her head. Cosima and her husband, the gloriously handsome property magnate arlo forrester, were as inseparable as ever.

Cosima kissed padme's cheek. "girl did good, pad. We're all so, so proud of you."

Padme flushed with pleasure. Cosima was the big sister padme had always wanted: kind, sweet, and generous. She smiled at her now. "number five, eh?"

Cosima nodded at arlo. "the spermanator."

Padme giggled as arlo rolled his eyes. "how are your other offspring?"

"tilly and fen are in paris on a school trip—delighted to be away from their nagging parents."

"typical eight-year-olds."

"yep. Mina is at her first sleepover and loving it, and bear is at home with the babysitter. They're exhausting," cosima said with an exaggerated groan, and a twinkle in her eye. Padme knew she loved being a mother as much as she loved being an architect. Cosima was a force of nature, managing to fit more in a day than most people did in a lifetime. She nodded to padme.

"excited about your first real assignment?"

Padme nodded. "nervous excitement. Dale, my partner, and i

are going to protect an italian businessman who pissed off the wrong people. He's going to testify against the ingles."

Arlo whistled. "brave dude—they are some nasty, nasty people."

"tell me about it. I've seen the photos of some of their victims—and worse, their victims' wives and children. So, i'm being thrown in the deep end here."

Cosima was frowning now. "it sounds dangerous, pad. You will be careful, won't you?"

Padme smiled at her friend gratefully. "i will."

"did severin make it tonight?"

Severin was padme's sort-of-adopted-mother, if it was possible to be sort of adopted at eighteen. Severin had come into padme's life at a time when she needed a mentor, someone to help steer her away from the life of misery and degradation that had been beckoning. Severin banks was one of seattle's most prominent activists. At age sixty-four, she showed no signs of stopping—her campaigns for equal pay for women, for the lgbt community, and for the advancement of her own black community kept her in the headlines. When she had seen the young, lost, almost destitute half-indian girl, she had taken her under her wing, and had inspired padme to be the change she wanted to see.

Padme shook her head. "she has a date."

Cosima chuckled. "with the same guy as last time?"

"nah, that fizzled out. This guy is nice, a lot younger. Severin says it's a good thing; he'll have enough stamina to keep up with her."

Cosima and arlo laughed, and they chatted a little longer before cosima was stolen away by her sister as harpa made a small speech, thanking everyone for coming.

Padme refilled her drink and circulated, using her finely-tuned observation skills to engage in some people-watching. It was just after midnight when she felt someone staring at her. She glanced up, and her insides went to mush. Across the room, the most gorgeous man was smiling at her. He was tall, casually dressed in a light white linen top and jeans, leaning back against the wall. His dark hair was shaggy and wild about his head, his smile sensual and confident.

Padme felt that smile everywhere. She sipped her drink, unable to tear her gaze away from his. He pushed himself away from the wall and walked slowly toward her. Padme's heart began to pound.

A second later, she cursed silently as one of harpa's friend's descended on her, arms open. What was her name again? Deirdre? Brenda? "darling pad," she breathed, enveloping her in a warm hug. "i just heard you graduated. Congratulations, sweetie! Come, let me buy you an enormous drink and you can tell me all about the fbi."

Padme smiled at the woman. She really was very sweet; it was just that her timing sucked. The sexy god had disappeared, obviously moved on to a more available target. Damn it. Padme was feeling in need of a little male attention. The initial sexual attraction some of her male classmates had felt for her had either turned into friendship, or as she progressed and they saw how brilliant she was and how much better she was at the job than they were, resentment. Padme didn't care one iota. She had one hard and fast rule: never pee in the company pool. Ever.

She was still a woman with needs though, and she knew once she got into her new assignment, she would be focused solely on that ... and all work, and no play, she thought now, with a grin to herself. Deirdre/brenda was talking about her kids now and padme nodded along politely, still scanning the room, looking for him.

Her companion drifted away after a few minutes and harpa

came over to replenish padme's drink. "did you get caught?" She asked with a grin, "barbara's lovely, but she can talk for hours."

Barbara, that was it. Padme chuckled. "she's sweet. Hey, harp, who's the guy with the dark curls, very sexy, tall?"

Harpa looked blank. "mikah?"

Padme laughed. "no, doofus." She looked around and spotted him at the bar. "him, there."

Harpa followed her line of sight. "oh, him. Yes, god, isn't he something else? No one seems to know who he is."

"a crasher?"

"maybe, but when they look like that, they can crash all they want." Harpa grinned at padme. "you should go for it, pad. You need some r&r."

Padme smirked. "i don't think i'd be resting and relaxing if i had a man like that."

"well, in his case, it would stand for riding and reaming."

Padme nearly choked on her drink. "that is so gross, harpa malhotra."

"you would, though."

"i would."

"is that mikah waving like a loon at me? Excuse me, pad, he's having a crisis."

Harpa disappeared—and so had the r&r guy again. Elusive bastard, wasn't he? Still, despite giggling over harpa's coarseness, she let herself fantasize about the man's cock being inside her, fucking her hard … god, she was getting wet just thinking about it.

The drink was definitely getting to her. The music had been turned down to a slow sensual beat now, the lighting had dimmed, and people were beginning to dance.

Padme closed her eyes, listening to the music. She felt a fingertip being lightly traced down her spine and knew instantly it was him. She felt his hands on her waist as he turned her to face him. Her eyes still closed, not wanting to break the spell, she felt his lips brush her eyelids lightly.

"hello." Soft, deep, sensual.

Padme opened her eyes and looked into the greenest eyes she had ever seen, locked on hers intently. Neither of them spoke; they just gazed at each other for the longest time. Then he slipped a hand onto the small of her back and began to dance with her. Their bodies swayed in time with the music, getting closer and closer. Padme couldn't look away from his intense gaze, her body responding to him. He pulled her closer, his lips an inch from hers, but he made no attempt to kiss her, the anticipation of it both sweet and painful.

Padme traced the shape of his lips with a trembling finger, then stroked his face. He really was achingly handsome. His hand was on her belly now, stroking it through the thin silk of her dress and padme felt herself relax into his touch, wanting more. She could feel the hardness of his erection through his jeans; it, too, pressed against her belly. He tangled his hands in her hair and finally, finally, his lips met hers. A rush of heady sensations shot through padme and she moaned softly as he kissed her. She heard him chuckle, a low, deep, sexy sound.

"beautiful girl," he whispered, his lips at her ear, "i want you so badly, i want to be in you, right now ..."

Padme could only nod, god, yes, yes, she wanted this man to fuck her now, please ...

"come with me," he said softly and took her hand. She let herself be led out of the main room into the corridor at the back of the restaurant. His hand felt so good, the fingers warm and dry, and she couldn't help imagining them on her breasts, her belly, stroking her clit ...

What the actual hell? Am i actually going to do this? In public? She blinked back into reality and stopped. "wait."

He turned to her, his hands on her waist now. "for what?" He asked, his voice low and sexy, american—or at least trying to sound american. His eyes were merry, filled with desire for her, and padme felt weak.

He bent his head, and as his lips touched hers, all reason fled and she kissed him back with as much passion as he did her. His hands tangled in her long dark hair, bunching it up in his fist as he pushed her against the wall of the hallway.

Padme gasped as his hands slid under her dress and pushed it up, his fingers stroking her through her panties. God, yes ... the mere force of him, his machismo, his hard body ...

He dropped to his knees, tugging her panties from her, and then his tongue was on her clit. Padme gasped, a little shocked, but her mysterious lover didn't relent, bringing her to the point of a shattering orgasm before standing and pulling her into an unlocked office.

"i need to hear you moan," he said, locking the door after them. "and i need to hear you scream when you come."

Jesus, this man. He swept her off of her feet and laid her on the desk. Padme pulled her dress over her head and he pulled down a lacy cup of her bra and took her nipple into his mouth.

She cupped his cock through his jeans, stroking the hot, massive length of it. He smiled at her and then the frenzy began, him almost biting at her in his desperate need for her, padme freeing his rampant cock from his pants.

She took him into her mouth and teased the tip of his cock with her tongue, stroking the length of him with her fingers, massaging his balls. He would not let her suck him for long; he drew away and pulled her legs around him. Padme almost cried at the anticipation of it, and when his cock slammed deep into her, she cried out, laughing and moaning. Her lover smiled down at her as he thrust, their bodies fitting together so perfectly, they found a rhythm easily. Padme moaned at the feel of him plunging deep into her, clinging to him as he supported her. They fucked hard, not caring if they were caught, completely focused on the other. He was so beautiful she could barely stand to look at him, his green eyes fixed on hers, their connection one of pure desire.

Padme came, muffling her cries in his neck as she felt him come, pumping thick creamy cum deep into her belly. Her vagina contracted hard around his pumping cock, taking him in, milking him. God ... was this stupid and reckless? Probably, but she didn't care at this particular moment. He caressed her clit, making stars explode in her visions, the feeling of not caring if she lived or died making her delirious. When he finally withdrew, he buried his face in her soft belly, kissing it, rimming her navel with his tongue. He was still wearing his linen top, but padme had slid her fingers under it and was now stroking his hard and finely-honed torso. He was so broad, so masterful, his body completely dominating hers. He kissed her again, the embrace full of tenderness.

They caught their breaths, panting hard, gazing at the other. "that was incredible," she whispered, and he gave a low, sexy chuckle.

"yes, it was. But i have a feeling the best is yet to come. Come back to my hotel with me, beautiful one."

And padme couldn't think of one reason to say no.

SHE QUICKLY RETURNED to the main room and hugged harpa goodbye, trying not to think of the sexy man waiting for her outside in a cab. He was leaning against it, grinning at her as she came to meet him. God, this was ... there wasn't a word for it. Insane? She didn't even know his name, and yet it seemed right to go with him.

He kissed her all the way to his hotel, not caring what the cab driver thought, or the people in the elevator on the way up to his room. Padme was completely under his spell, and when they finally reached his room, he began to pull her dress off, apparently eager to get her naked as soon as possible.

His hands on her skin made padme's heart race. His tongue caressed hers before he freed her breasts from her bra, and then his mouth was on each of her nipples in turn, sucking and teasing until they were so sensitive she could have screamed. Instead, she tugged his shirt over his head, and as her hands worked the zipper of his jeans she explored his chest with her mouth, trailing her lips across his hard pecs, biting down gently on his nipples. His cock was hot and huge in her hands, diamond-hard and quivering as she stroked it.

Her lover gave a growl of pure desire and carried her to the bed, laying her down and pushing her knees to her chest before slamming his cock into her. He pinned her hands above her head, his gloriously handsome face intensely focused on hers as they fucked, his mouth almost savage as he kissed her.

Padme gasped and moaned through two orgasms, and when he finally released her hands, she cupped his face with her palms, watching as his orgasm hit. His face became softer with the release. He gave a long groan, his cock pumping thick streams of cum deep inside her.

He kissed her as he withdrew, but padme wanted more. She moved down his body and took his still-half-erect cock into her mouth, the silky skin salty with his cum. She traced the vein up the side, feeling his cock engorge with blood again. His hands gently stroked her hair as she brought him to the brink of another orgasm before he pulled her on top of him. She rode him hard, slamming her hips against his as his hands cupped her breasts.

They fucked twice more before collapsing on the bed exhausted, panting for air. After a moment, they looked at each other and began to laugh.

"well," he said softly. "hello."

Padme grinned at him. "hello ... and lose that american accent, would you? So far, it's the only fake thing about you."

He chuckled. "fair point." He rolled onto his side and kissed her. "well, then, hello. I'm danilo."

Okay, so her finely-tuned fbi training told her he was still lying, but maybe that was okay for now. She'd seen enough of him to know he wasn't carrying a concealed weapon, she grinned to herself. His sexy italian accent made her want to look past just about anything, especially a little white lie. "penny," she said, giving him a look that told him two can play that game, buddy.

Danilo smiled. "i didn't expect to go to a party and meet the most beautiful woman i have ever seen."

Her mouth hitched up on one side. "that's such a line."

"no, it's true, but i can see your point. You don't have to trust me."

Padme studied him. His face was both beautiful and rugged, a strange combination—she could imagine, when angry, he could look hard and dangerous. But now, she saw no threat in his looks—especially when he was looking at her like he wanted to fuck her senseless ... again.

"what's your real name?" She asked, taking a risk. His face grew pensive then, but he was no more willing to tell her the truth.

"i cannot tell you, principessa. It would be dangerous."

Padme felt a frisson go through her. "for whom?"

"for both of us."

Who was this dude? Was he a player who was trying to project an air of mystery? She studied him, trying to push past the crazy sex fog that came with thoroughly and expertly being fucked by a seriously sexy man, to see the person underneath. He grinned at her scrutiny. "you like what you see?"

Padme smothered a grin. He was so cheeky, so obviously fun-loving, that she couldn't quite reconcile that with his warning of potential danger. "who are you?"

He shrugged. "no one of importance."

"hmm." She kissed him, enjoying the feel of his lips against hers. He tasted so good. As she reluctantly pulled away, she fixed him with a mock-serious look. "now, i believe the proper thing to say at this point is that i don't normally do this kind of thing. The one-night thing. But i'm glad i did it with you."

He ran a hand down her body. "me too, cara mia. Believe it or not, i don't usually act with that much spontaneity—rather, i don't get the opportunity or have the desire to act that way. It wasn't a plan, it really was just you. You can believe that or not."

Padme decided she did believe him and kissed him. He smiled. "sweet one ... would you spend the weekend with me? I have to work from monday—or rather, i'm going to be somewhat absent from public life for a while. I would love to spend the next couple of days with you, if you don't have any prior commitments?"

Padme hesitated. She had planned on preparing for her first assignment on monday, getting some time in at the gym. If she were sensible she would leave now, before it got complicated, before she got too involved with someone who, by his own admission, would be gone by next week. Someone who might be dangerous. No. She would say goodnight now and leave it as a very, very pleasant memory. Be sensible. Don't risk your career over a handsome man. Good girl, she told herself.

"i'd love to stay," her mouth betrayed her.

Oh,

CHAPTER TWO

Frederick ingles waited while the airport staff brought the ladder to his private jet. He'd never been to seattle before, and he wasn't in the mood for sightseeing now. He hated to be dragged away from his paris home, especially for something as ridiculous as this, but enver toscano could bring down his entire world, and ingles was not about to allow that.

He got into the waiting limousine to see his private investigator waiting for him. "where is he?"

"hotel. With some whore he picked up. They haven't left his room all weekend."

Frederick's bodyguard wes spoke up. "seems ideal for a hit. Kill him, kill the girl—we could even make it look like a murder-suicide. Paint her as a crazy-obsessed chick."

Frederick rolled his eyes. "except we don't know who she is and her family or friends could ruin that plan. Besides, we had to register a flight plan—the fbi know i'm here. How quickly do you think they'll come for me if toscano and some random girl end up dead as soon as i fly in? Think, idiot."

He stared out of the window. "no, we play the long game. See if we can avoid any violence, for now. Intimidate toscano into keeping his mouth shut."

"probably shouldn't have offed his business partner then," wes muttered but was quelled under frederick's furious glare.

"wesley, when this trip is over, i want you to take some time. Think about if you really want to defy me at every turn. Now, shut up."

Wesley shut up. Frederick sighed. The murder of maximillian nero had been unfortunate but necessary, and frederick had underestimated enver toscano's grief for his friend and his determination for revenge. Even threatening one of enver's girlfriends hadn't stopped him from vowing to bring the ingles down, and the girlfriend had been quietly whisked away somewhere they couldn't touch her.

The ingles family ruled most of europe. France, italy, spain, germany—there were very few countries that their malevolent presence didn't reach. Their business—money laundering –was run under the guise of philanthropy and their enemies were dealt with ruthlessly and efficiently.

Until max nero had uncovered the evidence of their dealings, the ingles had run roughshod over their competition, the police, even interpol. Nothing and no one could touch them.

Frederick shook his head, remembering the day he'd killed max. A mistake. It had been frederick's first misstep since taking over as head of the company after his father's death. He should have paid off max instead of killing him. Max was malleable, unlike enver. Max had given him the option.

If only fred had listened to max before he offed him. His words came back now to taunt him: "believe me, frederick, this is a better deal for you. If enver ever found this information … you may think he's the playboy in this, that he'd rather fuck your wife than use this information, but you should never, ever underestimate him. He's a good man, through and through. Any whiff of corruption and he'll bring the force of law down on you. And then he'll fuck your wife, and she'll swear blind, even under the threat of death, that he was the best lover she'd ever known."

Frederick had snarled, losing his temper, and ordered max killed. He was aware the second he had killed max and his wife, julia—and not quickly either—that it was the wrong move. Enver would mourn the loss of his friend and be like a tenacious puppy. It hadn't taken enver long before he'd found out what happened—some jerk wad on frederick's staff had sold the ingles out. Enver had vowed to bring them down—frederick had expected a bullet. But what enver wanted was the destruction of the ingles' family business; he wouldn't be satisfied by the simple death of one of the ingles. He went to the fbi and told them he would testify under oath and destroy the ingles' reputation once of for all.

Which meant that now frederick would have to kill enver toscano, and soon. Whoever this girl was, frederick hoped she was only a one-night stand, because he hated to kill an innocent woman. He smirked to himself. No, you love it, you sick fuck, just admit it. He shrugged. He didn't really care about this girl who was fucking toscano.

But no one would get in the way of enver toscano's murder.

No one.

EXHAUSTED AND SATED—FOR now, at least—danilo ordered room service, and they lounged around in fluffy white robes, sharing french fries and burgers and fresh fruit. Padme's body ached and she was tired but elated. Making love with danilo, she could barely believe they had only just met. He grinned at her now.

"you have the most adorable blush on your cheeks." He

stroked a finger down one, then laughed as padme pretended to bite it. She sighed happily and leaned back against the couch.

"so, tell me about yourself. What you can, of course." She still desperately wanted to know why he thought telling her anything about him, even his name, would be dangerous, but she didn't want to ruin the atmosphere.

"hmm," he said, "well, i guess i can you i'm italian."

"big shocker." She pulled a face and he laughed.

"okay, then i can tell you … that i'd really like to fuck you again right now."

Padme made a show of crossing her legs. "not until i get more information, buddy."

He trailed his fingers along her thigh. "really?"

"really." She giggled as he gently parted her legs and began to stroke her clit again. It responded immediately. "oh, goddamn it, man, just give me something."

He pulled open his robe and she saw his cock was already hard, standing proud and huge against his belly. Padme felt her sex dampen but she looked at him disapprovingly. "if you can't tell me your real first name … how about your middle name? That won't tell me anything."

He was pushing her back on the couch now, pulling open her robe, kissing from her throat downwards. "lucio."

"lucio, lucio … i'm gonna smoochio with lucio," she said and grinned as he groaned at her bad joke.

"just for that, you're going to get this," and he thrust his tumescent cock into her, hard, "and this … and this …" harder and deeper, he fucked her into submission, and padme forgot all the questions she had. He took her on the floor, on the couch, even in the shower.

LATER, padme told him a little about her past. "i was born here, but for the first five years of my life, i was raised in india. We came back here when my mom got a job, but she soon found it too hard to keep me and she gave me up for adoption when i was five."

Danilo looked appalled. "god, that must have been horrific."

"well, yes, kind of. She wasn't the warmest of mothers, or the most loving. At first, in the children's home, they were kind, but when they realized no one would adopt a mixed race five-year-old, they soon became tired of me, and i of them. I wasn't the best behaved either. When i was thirteen, a guardian molested me. No one believed me, of course, so i ran away and lived on the streets for about three years, until severin found me and took me in. I worked a lot of part-time jobs to pay for college and i turned my life around."

"penny, i'm so sorry. What do you do now?" He seemed genuinely interested in her life but suddenly padme was uncomfortable. She didn't want to tell him she was fbi—it might freak him out.

"i'm in criminal psychology." It was near enough to the truth so she didn't feel bad.

"that must be fascinating and disturbing in equal measure."

She smiled at him gratefully. "you can say that again." Her mind flitted back to the photographs she'd been sent earlier that week. A murdered mother and her as-yet unborn, near-full-term child. He had been cut from his mother's womb and killed. The mother had been butchered. So much blood, so much cruelty. She tried to push away the thought of robert, her abuser from her childhood, threatening padme's life. She would never forget his face as he held a knife to her. Tell anyone, kid, and i'll gut you.

She shivered and danilo frowned. "are you okay?"

"bad memories."

He gathered her to him, holding her so tenderly she thought she might cry. "i will try to erase those bad times, if you let me."

She smiled, stroking back his dark hair. "i have no doubt you would. Enough about me. At least tell me about your home in italy. You don't have to go into specifics, but describe the countryside, the towns. I've always wanted to go."

"well," he said, "it's tuscany. You've seen the photographs. Rolling hills, villas on hilltops, cypress trees, olive groves. It's all there. And yes, i do love it, more than anywhere else. I think you would like it. I would very much like to take you there one day."

Padme felt uncomfortable. "danilo, i'm not looking for a long-term relationship, right now. Not that you totally wouldn't be worth it, but i've just gotten my life to how i want it to be. Work, home ..." she trailed off, sensing she'd hurt him. "although, of course, i would love to go to italy."

Danilo was studying her. "i have no expectations, penny, none. It was an off-hand comment, but i meant it. Even if we are not ... lovers, i hope we will always be friends."

"that, at least, i can promise you, i think," she said cautiously. She placed her palm against his cheek. "you have made this last day unbelievably fun and exciting and blissful."

He rolled her onto her back, burying his head in her neck. "and you too. You may not believe me, but i don't usually have this kind of connection. I admit, last night, my thoughts were solely on fucking you senseless."

"which you achieved and then some," she grinned, then sighed as he pulled her legs around his waist again, gliding his cock into her. "god, this is truly heavenly, danilo, but it feels too good to be true, as well."

Danilo kissed her thoroughly. "for this weekend, at least, can't it be?"

And she couldn't think of one single reason why it shouldn't.

. . .

In the hotel across the street from enver toscano's hotel, frederick ingles watched the couple making love. He had to give it the man: toscano chose well; the girl was stunning. All dark hair and dusky. He lowered the binoculars and stepped away from the window, his cock hard against his pants. Maybe he would kill the girl too, make toscano watch as he, frederick, gutted her slowly. Yes, that would be good.

Tonight, though, his fingers itched for the kill. With his looks, frederick ingles could get anyone. Yes, he had a wife back home, a wife whom he adored and hated in equal measure and she, him, but he wouldn't dream of sating his darkest desires on her.

No. He preferred taking a random beauty from the streets, fucking her until she cried, then killing her slowly. That was what he needed tonight. He picked up his phone.

"wesley? Did you arrange the kill room here in seattle? I will need it tonight." He listened with satisfaction to wesley's affirmation. "good. Go prepare it, and arrange for the clean-up afterward."

It took him two hours to find the one he wanted. Soft looking, wide eyed and innocent was how he liked them. Naïve. Vulnerable. She was a beauty too, not unlike toscano's whore, dusky-skinned and lush. She was easily seduced, then easily subdued. He fucked her, fully clothed, then strangled her until she lost consciousness. He laid her on the bed, on top of the plastic sheeting, and ripped open the bodice of her dress. When she came around, he slowly pushed the knife into her belly again and again until she had bled out. Her lovely eyes were open and staring, her body limp. She had died too quickly, but that couldn't be helped. His cock was hard and that was all he wanted.

He left the girl's body and went back to his hotel, jerking off in the shower as he rinsed the blood away. He relived the killing, imagining that it had been toscano's whore he was murdering, her belly yielding to his lethal knife over and over. Yes, he would kill her. It would be her punishment for screwing enver toscano.

Frederick ingles smiled as he came, imagining the light leaving the beautiful girl's eyes as he killed her.

Padme tried not to show how miserable she felt as sunday night came around. She never, ever thought she would be dreading this particular monday morning, but the last forty-eight hours had been nothing short of … magical.

Danilo—or whatever his name was—wasn't just a phenomenal lover. He was incredibly funny, sweet, and fascinating. He told her what he could about his past—born and raised in florence, italy, by his italian father and american mother, he had lost both of them young, his father when he was five, his mother when he was just eighteen. His best friend, max, had died recently and danilo was still raw from it.

Padme marveled at his ability to wear his heart on his sleeve. It made the conversation between them easy and fun and above all else, it felt genuine. Often, she thought about telling him about who she was, asking him to trust her to tell her his real name. She wanted to know … him. The real him. His name was important.

Now, she wondered why she had worried about it. Their connection had been deeper than mere names or even sex, as great as it was.

And now, she was going to have to say goodbye, and she was struggling to find the words.

"hey," danilo came from the bathroom—a white towel wrapped around his body. They had just showered together, making love under the spray of hot water. His dark curls were damp against his face, his eyes such a beautiful color against his tanned skin. Padme ran her eyes over his body, not bothering to hide her admiration.

"dude, you are one gorgeous man."

Danilo grinned. "why, thank you." He came to the bed and covered her body with his. "as long as you think so." He was already hard, and padme pulled the towel away from his hips.

"that's better. You should always be naked."

They laughed. "that would make business meetings difficult, but intriguing. How about we make a deal? If i'm naked, you're naked."

She kissed him. "deal."

He kissed her back, tenderly, as if memorizing the shape of her lips, and then buried his face in her neck, making a strange growling sound. "mio dio, i don't want to let you go," he murmured, and padme felt her chest ache. No, neither did she —she wanted to hang onto him, to them, to these last few moments together.

He looked up and she saw the genuine conflict in his eyes. "hey," she said softly. "we said one weekend. And it's been perfect. I mean it ... these have been the most incredible few days."

Danilo nuzzled her nose with his. "they have. I just wish ..." he sighed. "i wish that i wasn't who i was, that i could just be here with you and not have to deal with ..." he didn't finish the sentence, just looked at her sadly. "i've never met anyone like you before. And it would have to happen now."

Padme swept her hands over his face, gazing up at him. "my name isn't penny."

He grinned that crooked smile she was quickly coming to love. "i know. And you know i'm not danilo."

"yes."

He kissed her. "soon, i hope i'll be free to tell you my real name."

"just whisper it to me," she pleaded. "i swear on my life, it will go no further." She saw the hesitation in his eyes. "to sweeten the deal ... my real name is padme kaur."

"that's beautiful." She could see the conflict in his eyes.

"trust me," she said simply, and he nodded.

"you're about the only person in the world i do trust, even after this short time. But if i tell you my name and one day you slip—we are only human—then it could mean your life being in danger. I want to tell you so much, padme, i really, really do. Please just trust me enough to say, when it's safe—i'll tell you everything."

And she had to be satisfied with that. They made love again and then, just after midnight, padme said goodbye to the most sensual man she'd ever met. She traveled by cab back to her apartment and, opening the door, she dumped her purse on the table and stood for a long minute in silence before bursting into tears.

CHAPTER THREE

"Why do you look so grumpy?" Dale, her partner, squinted at her as she got into his car the next morning.

"mind your own business," she snapped before relenting. "sorry, d. I had a weird weekend."

Dale grinned at her. "bet i can cheer you up. Guess who got the cleveland posting?"

Padme suddenly perked up. "tell me it was maria. Please tell me it was maria."

"bingo." They both cheered, and dale was right, that did perk padme's spirits up. Maria had been at quantico with them—an arrogant, incompetent know-it-all who delighted in telling them that her father had been an agent for thirty-five years and she knew it all by osmosis. She didn't. Couple her annoying attitude with her abject jealousy over padme's brilliance, and maria had been the focus of most of the class's hatred. Now she had been posted to the least-requested field office in the states.

"i have to admit, as much as it makes me a bad person ... well, that's karma, bitch," padme was grinning now. Dale chuckled.

"see, told you i could cheer you up. God, this traffic today. All ready for our babysitting job?"

Padme rolled her eyes. "guess we can't be too picky right out of the academy. Who is this guy?"

"no idea. We get our orders from the office, then head out."

HENRY JONES GREETED them both with a smile. "welcome, welcome. Not to blow smoke up your asses right off the bat, but we hit pay dirt with you two. You know every field office was clamoring for you?"

Padme and dale looked at each other, not knowing what to say. Henry grinned. "well, now that we have the good news out of the way ... here comes the real world. You may think we're just handing you a babysitting job, but this guy is putting it all on the line to bring down the ingles, and we're going to have his back while he's doing it. The death threats are real, and this kid, enver toscano, has already seen his business partner murdered. Also, frederick ingles flew into seattle on saturday. He knows where toscano was this weekend, but since then, we've transferred toscano to a safe house. You read the briefing notes? Good."

He sat on the edge of the desk. "his lawyer, an arrogant asshole called brian dedalus, specifically requested new agents. The ingles have spies everywhere, and he is betting on them not having gotten to you two—yet. So, get over to this address. You'll meet the lawyer and the protectee, and work out the protection detail together. Don't forget to brief me about what you decide."

He stopped talking and studied them. "we're throwing you in the deep end, kids. Look after yourselves."

DALE AND PADME were quiet as they drove to the safehouse, realizing just how much responsibility they had been handed. Padme drove while dale looked over the case file.

"jesus, this guy's young to be in this situation. Thirty-seven and a multi-billionaire. Single, workaholic, playboy. The usual. Stepping up to the plate, though."

Padme smiled at him. "you getting a crush on the protectee? Gonna be his best buddy?"

Dale grinned. "screw you, kaur."

"you wish."

"shut up."

Even though they spent the journey busting each other's chops, both were still on high alert, constantly checking to make sure they weren't followed. Padme even erred on the side of caution when she saw a sedan with blacked-out windows pull alongside their suv. She turned off the highway and took a detour, but the sedan was long gone.

They arrived at the safe house and were greeted by a security team. After showing their ids, they were led into the house. A young woman, thin in the extreme with long blonde hair and nervous energy, smiled shyly at them. "hi, i'm chaley, mr. Toscano's personal assistant. Please come this way. He and mr. Dedalus are waiting to meet you."

They were led down a long, lushly carpeted corridor. Even if this was a safehouse, enver toscano obviously wanted to be kept in comfort. Padme caught dale's eye, and he smirked, apparently thinking the same thing.

Chaley led them into a room where a smartly-dressed man sat on a large couch, a briefcase by his side and a laptop open. He looked up, and padme saw his ice-blue eyes take them in.

"where the fuck have you been? We were told you would be here by ten a.m."

Padme looked at the man coolly. His hair was artfully swept back and held in place, padme was almost certain, by a butt-load of hairspray. His blue eyes were cold, and his manner was one of arrogance and entitlement—in other words, an asshole. Was this the protectee? If so, he could just go fu ... "we were told to make sure we arrived here safely and unseen. Which is what we did. Now, how about you try that again?"

The man stood—padme was amused to see he was smaller than her five-feet-nine-inches—and flushed angrily. "fine. Well, now that you're finally here ..."

"let's start over. I'm agent kaur; this is agent fortuna. Are you enver toscano?"

"no, he's not," said a beautifully accented and very familiar voice behind her. "i'm enver toscano."

With a jolt and a pounding heart, padme turned to see the man whose magnificent cock, a mere twenty-four hours earlier, had been deep inside her as he made her scream with pleasure again and again

From his expression, enver toscano was as shocked to see her as she was to see him. This was the man whose life was in danger? God, no, please, not him. Suddenly everything made sense. To his credit, he immediately covered his surprise and shook both their hands.

"thank you for coming. Do excuse brian; he's not had his ritalin this morning."

Padme smothered a snort of laughter with a cough. Enver invited them to sit, managing to squeeze padme's fingers inconspicuously. He was dressed in jeans and a vintage t-shirt, and padme wondered how she could ever have thought the slimeball lawyer dedalus was enver.

Enver was careful not to stare at her, but as they talked, padme was hyper-aware of his body close to hers, his eyes on hers when she spoke. She felt like she was stammering and gibbering like an idiot as she outlined the protection plan she and dale had come up with, but the men in the room seemed to nod along with it just fine. Even dedalus looked appeased.

"obviously," dale took over from her, "when it's time to transport you to the courtroom, we've arranged a decoy vehicle. We'll actually be flying you via helicopter to the helipad nearest the courtroom, and then more decoy cars will be sent out as we transfer you by car. We're taking this very seriously, mr. Toscano."

Enver nodded. "and i couldn't be more grateful for your help."

"so, one of you will always be here with us?" Brian dedalus looked at dale and then raked his eyes up and down padme's body, apparently considering how a slim woman like her could protect a six-foot-two man like enver. His judgment made her bristle with annoyance—he really was an asshole—henry hadn't exaggerated.

"yes," she said, her voice hardening. "and i will have to remind you that any and all decisions regarding mr. Toscano's movements must be discussed with us."

She felt dale nudge her discreetly and then he cleared his throat. "agent kaur is the lead on this, so she has the final say on any decision."

Padme tried not to look surprised—they hadn't discussed who would lead and she was grateful to dale for his support. If brian dedalus thought he could pull any misogynistic crap on her, he had another think coming.

Enver was watching her, his eyes amused. "in that case, perhaps, agent fortuna, you can go brief my security team with brian, and i can settle things with agent kaur."

"call me dale, and yeah, that's a good idea." Dale looked at padme, who nodded at him, a smile on her flushed, burning face—at least it felt like it was burning.

When dale and dedalus had left, enver smiled at chaley. "chaley, would you mind giving us a minute? Take a break, get yourself a coffee."

Chaley hopped off the end of the sofa, shooting enver and padme a smile—and then finally, they were alone.

Padme let out a long breath. "enver toscano."

Enver came to her side, sweeping a loose strand of hair back over her ear. "mio dio, padme, i can't say it isn't good to see you, but the thought of you putting yourself in harm's way for me …"

"i would take a bullet for you in a heartbeat," she whispered fiercely, "but it's not going to get to that, enver. I won't let anyone hurt you."

His lips were against hers then, and for a moment, she fantasized that this could be their reality. She drew away after a moment. "but we can't do this. Not if i'm going to protect you properly. If i get distracted and something happens to you … god, enver."

"and i cannot bear the thought that you might get hurt because of me. This is just what i was trying to avoid." He got up and paced around the room. "maybe we should … ask for a replacement?"

"no." Padme felt panicked. "no. I won't be able to trust anyone else to protect you the way i would. I meant what i said. This is my job, enver. It's my job to put myself in front of any bullet meant for you and that's what i'll have to do if i have to."

Enver's eyes were sad. "you don't even know me, padme, cara mia."

Padme stood and went to him. "i do know you. I know you love with your whole heart, that the loss of someone close to you could crush you. I feel the same way—about you. I know that's completely the opposite of what a woman is supposed to say after the weekend we had—i'm supposed to act cool, and in our case, god knows, professionally, but … i don't trust anyone else to protect you. It doesn't matter that we haven't known each other long; i know that i don't want anything bad to happen to you."

Enver kissed her gently. "the moment this is over, padme kaur, you and i are going to spend a lot of time together. Naked. I think we agreed to that on the weekend. Deal?"

She smiled. "deal." Her voice was a whisper. How had her life changed this much in such a short amount of time?

They heard dale and brian returning. "don't mind brian," enver said in a low voice. "he just wants this over and done with so he can get back to his life in new york."

"he's staying here?"

Enver rolled his eyes. "he doesn't trust me to be by myself."

"you're not."

Enver met her gaze as the others came back into the room. "hopefully i won't be alone ever again, my beautiful padme."

He said it in a low voice, but it sent padme's heart into overdrive. She knew she should tell dale and her bosses of her relationship with enver, however humiliating that might be, but she was convinced that no one could protect enver better than she would.

CHALEY SHOWED dale and padme to their respective rooms, dale whistling in appreciation at the comfortable beds and widescreen television. Padme dumped her hold-all on the bed and wondered how she could possibly sleep knowing enver was only a few rooms away. God, how she wanted him, but she would not compromise his safety for the sake of a fuck—even if that fuck was with the most gorgeous man she'd ever met. Padme knew that if they risked it and were discovered, she would be fired and maybe even arrested for compromising the operation.

There was a soft knock at her door, and her heart began to

thump. "come in." She was both relieved and disappointed when dale opened the door, giving her a boyish grin.

"hey you, just wanted to know if you want me to take the night shift. You look kind of done in already."

Padme smiled at him. "and it's only lunchtime. No, it's okay, i'm kind of a night owl. I'll take the late shift."

Dale flopped down on the bed next to her. "what do you think of him?"

"enver? Nice guy. Good for him taking on the ingles."

Dale nodded. "that's what i think. That lawyer, though." They both laughed. "by the look of him, he's read american psycho once too often."

Padme snorted. "he's not that interesting. He does know the eighties are over, right?"

"you're such a bitch." But dale was laughing. Padme punched his arm and got up off the bed.

"come on, we have work to do."

4

CHAPTER FOUR

By the evening, they both realized that babysitting duty was as dull as it sounded. Brian dedalus ignored them, jabbering away on his cell phone. Chaley, shy and nervous, would offer them coffee every time she saw them. Enver was working, but would stop when he saw them and chat, and padme grew more impressed by him every time they talked. In sharp contrast to his lawyer, enver was humble and apologetic for having put them in this situation. But mostly, he was just fun and smart to be around.

As padme got to know him better over the next few days, she found herself feeling even more conflicted about their whole situation. Enver was everything she wanted, and everything she couldn't have. She took the night shifts, listening to the silence around the compound as she walked the corridors. Enver had taken to joining her, and they would sit and talk until dawn, each desperate to touch the other, but knowing they couldn't.

"when this is over," enver said, late one night a week after they'd come to the safehouse, "i would love to take you away, to italy, to show you my home."

"do you have any family left?"

"a few cousins scattered throughout the country. Claudio is the closest to me. He's an artist. His sister, soleil, died a few years ago."

Some memory pinged in padme's memory at the unusual name. "are you talking about soleil fonseca? The murder down in los angeles?" Enver nodded, his eyes sad. "god, that was horrific. I'm so sorry, enver."

"thank you. It was a bad time for us all, especially claudio."

Padme shook her head. "so much pain."

Enver smiled a little and covered her hand with his. "you make it better."

Padme's eyes locked on his and before she knew what was happening his lips were against hers. God, he was intoxicating. "we can't do this ..." she said, but then lost herself in the kiss. Enver pulled her into his arms and her body curved around his. "enver ... enver ..."

His hands were at the waistband of her pants, his eyes questioning. Despite what her brain was trying to tell her, she could not tell him to stop. There was a frenzy of stripping clothes as they ran their hands over each other's bodies and then enver was sliding his huge cock into her as they tumbled to the carpet. They fucked quickly, intensely, smothering their moans with their mouths, lips against lips, skin on skin.

Padme's legs tightened around his waist as he plowed deeper and deeper into her, her fingernails digging into the finely-honed muscles of his back. She came, dampening her cry of release by pressing her lips to his shoulder as enver buried his face in her neck to muffle his groan as he came with her.

They lay together, panting, listening for any sign that they had been heard. There was silence throughout the property. "god," padme said, her face flushed, her hair sticking to the sweat on her face. "we really shouldn't have done that."

Enver grinned down at her, not looking the least bit repentant. "i think it was kind of inevitable, cara mia."

She chuckled quietly. "you're so cocky. Help me up, big guy. I'm supposed to be protecting you."

He pulled her to her feet and they got dressed, pausing often to kiss. Enver persuaded her to go to the large kitchen with him, and they made sandwiches, falling on them as if they were half-starved.

"food and sex," enver grinned at her, "my two favorite things."

"keeping you alive, baby, is my favorite thing. Seriously, enver, that has to be the last time until the case is over."

Enver nodded, sobering up. "i know. I'm sorry, padme. I could not stop myself."

"don't apologize. I wanted you just as much—i still want you. Badly. But this is your life we're talking about."

"and yours," he said firmly. He set his sandwich down and ran a hand through his dark hair. "god, i'll be glad when this thing starts. The trial, i mean."

"the d.a. told me you'll actually be testifying against one of the ingles' associates? Not frederick ingles himself?"

Enver rolled his eyes. "they won't arrest freddy ingles himself; he's too important. Their words. They'll just take his knees out from beneath him. He has deals in place with many high-ranking government officials in europe, but the slightest whiff of corruption and they'll pull out of his deals. It will make his organization very hard to deal with."

Padme blinked. "i just don't get the business world. I guess i see things in black and white—you make a product, you sell the product. As soon as it gets more complicated than that, i'm out. I've never asked—what is your line of business?"

"shipping," enver said and grinned when she grimaced. "sexy, huh? Really, it was max who brought me on board. We had known each other since we were kids. After college, i was adrift, really—my major was in music—but i didn't know if i wanted to pursue it as a career. Max inherited his father's shipping business, and when i joined his company, i found i had a gift for negotiation. After i brokered a huge deal with the scandinavian governments, max made me a partner. His father had run a low-key operation, but we expanded it to become the world's biggest shipping company. I sound like a brochure."

Padme burst out laughing as he pulled a face at the end. "a little, but please, go on. Tell me more about max."

Enver smiled a little sadly. "he was my best friend, and i loved him, but he got greedy. Unbeknownst to me, he approached freddy ingles to broker a deal. The specifics of the deal, i don't know, but max came to me one night, telling me he'd gotten in too deep, that he had underestimated ingles' grip once he had max in his net. He told me a little about what he had discussed with ingles, but then ingles got nasty, threatening to kill max and everyone he loved if max reneged on the deal. Three days later, max and his wife, julia, were murdered in their home. They made max watch while they stabbed julia to death, and then cut max's throat. They came after me, but i'd been warned and wasn't where they expected." Enver let out a shaky breath. "julia was pregnant when they killed her"

"jesus." Padme felt a wave of horror flood over her. She didn't think she had processed how much enver's life was on the line until this moment. "enver ... if they're only going to hobble frederick's business, not arrest him, what's going to stop him from pursuing you for the rest of your life?"

Enver smiled sadly. "nothing. And i'm aware that once i testify, all bets are off. The fbi. Is under no obligation to keep protecting me."

Padme wanted to argue, but he was right. "god."

"i have been offered a pass into witness protection, but i don't want that."

Padme gazed at him, distressed. "if it keeps you alive, why not?"

There was a long pause. "because now i have someone who i cannot be parted from, padme, and they wouldn't let me see you again. I cannot live with that."

"oh, enver ..." padme felt her body go cold at the thought of it. She took a deep breath. "i can't be the reason you get killed. I can't."

"you wouldn't be. I'm saying i don't want my life curtailed by freddy ingles—and he is the one who would come after you as well as me. He's a sadist. Without him at the helm, the rest of them would crumble. They just want to be comfortable and get as much money as they can, without being bothered by scandal."

Padme chewed this over. "i wouldn't hesitate to put the asshole down. God, killing a pregnant woman?"

"and they knew it, too."

"cocksuckers," she spat. "just let me get a whiff of ingles, and i'll end him myself."

Enver's expression was hard. "i don't want you within a million miles of that psycho."

She gave him a lopsided grin. "it's kind of my job, enver."

He nodded, his expression concerned. "what made you go into the fbi, anyway?"

"i wanted to help people," she said simply. "it was either this or the military for me."

"did you go to college?"

She nodded. "a degree, then a master's in political science. When cosima ... wait, do you know cosima and arlo forrester?"

He nodded. "i do, a little."

"well, cosima was shot and seriously injured a few years ago by her fbi handler. We didn't know if she was going to make it. But because of it, the restrictions on protecting foreign nationals have been tightened up. I decided to join up to make sure they were, and now look where i am."

"isn't that what you call irony?" Enver grinned at her, but she shook her head.

"more like ... heartbreak. God, what am i doing?" Padme closed her eyes. "i've worked so hard to get where i am, enver; you don't know the half of it. Orphanage kid, mixed race, female. I've had to overcome a lot of discrimination to get here. If something happened to you, not just on my watch, but at all ... i don't think i could survive it."

Enver stroked her face. "i feel the same. And i don't want to compromise your career. That's not the kind of man i am."

Padme gazed at him. "you would be easy to fall in love with, enver toscano, but i can't risk it while your life is in danger."

He nodded. "and i won't risk anything happening to you, not for me. But know this ... i'm not done with you, padme kaur. Not at all."

THE TRIAL STARTED on a monday morning, three weeks after enver had been transferred to the safe house. Padme flew with enver in the helicopter, while dale and some other fbi agents organized the decoy vehicles. Padme's boss, henry, had insisted on coming with them, which padme was grateful for. She tried to put aside her terror that something would happen, that someone would get close enough to enver to hurt him, but she couldn't help feeling sick the whole journey to the courthouse.

Only when they stepped inside its heavily guarded confines did she allow her shoulders to un-bunch. She regarded every person she didn't know as a suspect, even some of the newly recruited agents. Henry smiled at her. "that's my girl," he said to her quietly, "always watching."

She nodded back at him. "do we have any intelligence of a

specific threat today?"

Henry shook his head. "we have eyes on ingles and his associates." He nodded at enver, who stood a little way away talking to brian dedalus. "how's it going with the protectee?"

Apart from wanting his cock inside me all day, every day, you mean? Padme swallowed a sudden giggle. "good. He's a smart guy, does what we want him to do." God, that didn't even cover it.

"big thing he's doing, taking them on all on his own. Brave guy."

Padme smiled. "yes."

She walked over to enver then, nodding at brian. "court says you're first up, enver."

He smiled at her. "so, maybe this will all be over soon?"

"doubtful," brian butted in. "your testimony could take days, even weeks." He looked at padme, his eyes cold. "wouldn't it be better to allow my client to live in a hotel adjacent to the court, rather than risk anything happening on the journey back and forth?"

Padme sighed inwardly. She really didn't like this joker. "local hotels would be the first place any assassin would look for enver. Yep, great idea."

She was rewarded by brian's face turning red. He excused himself, and they watched as he went to talk to henry. Enver chuckled. "he's gonna tell papa on you."

Padme shrugged, dismissive of the lawyer. "where on earth did you find that guy?"

"tinder," enver said with a straight face, and padme laughed.

"yeah, well, you should have swiped left."

"got it."

Padme looked at him. "you nervous?"

Enver nodded. "just want to get this show on the road."

"you'll nail it, baby." The epithet came out of her mouth

before she could stop it and enver smiled.

"i heard that."

"shut up," she hissed, and then laughed. A moment later, the court clerk called enver in. Padme watched him walk inside the courtroom and mouthed 'good luck' to him. He winked at her and disappeared into the courtroom.

Padme let out a sigh of relief. The public gallery in the courtroom had been shut off, and even the journalists covering the case had a gag order until enver was safely out of the country. There were armed guards in there with him—he was safe.

"hey." Dale came up behind her, and she turned. "we got him here alive. Feels pretty good, huh?"

Padme smiled. "sure does."

Dale grinned and lowered his voice. "he's a good guy, pads ... i'm really happy for you."

Her eyes widened, and she felt a cold fear spike inside her. "what?"

Dale put his hand on her arm. "don't worry, i'm not going to say a word, but it's pretty obvious to me that you two are ..."

"we are not anything," padme lied, "he's just a friendly guy." She hated to lie to dale like this, but she didn't want to risk being thrown off enver's case.

"girl, after everything we've been through, don't you think you can trust me? I'm not saying a word; i think it's a great thing. But you want to deny it, go right ahead."

Dale walked off, and padme felt awful. Dale was right—she should have trusted him. She caught up to him and pulled him into a corridor. "i'm sorry, d. You're right, enver and i have ... history. But we're not together, at least, not while this case is going on. It's too risky for him. For us."

Dale's expression softened. "i know. Listen, i meant what i said. I won't say a word. And hey, just for the record, you're a great agent. End of discussion."

Padme relaxed. "you are the best."

"oh, i know."

ENVER LOOKED DRAINED after a day's worth of questioning, and he was quiet on the trip back to the compound. Padme, sitting next to him, surreptitiously squeezed his hand and he gave her a weary smile.

"bad day?" She said, but he shook his head.

"no, just draining. They talked a lot about max and julia's murders. They showed the court photographs of the crime scene ... and their bodies."

"oh god, enver, i'm sorry."

He nodded, and she could see the pain in his eyes. She wanted so much to hold him, kiss him, make him feel comforted, but in this small confined helicopter, it was impossible without being seen by the pilot.

They landed back at the compound. The lights in the main house were out, and padme narrowed her eyes, feeling suspicious. They had left chaley and two security guards at the property. Padme drew her weapon. "enver, stay inside the copter with mac and wiley. Mac, if you hear shots, take off and go to the emergency safehouse. Got it?"

"got it, boss."

Enver leaned forward. "what is it?"

"probably nothing, but dale and i and the rest will do a sweep. I'll come get you as soon as we give the all clear."

She stepped out of the helicopter, but enver grabbed her hand. "stay safe, principessa," he whispered, and she nodded.

Padme and dale entered first, guns drawn, flashlights on. Padme flicked the lights on at the main switch, and the whole house lit up. There was silence. "chaley? Chaley sanders? Gary holder? Kevin?"

There was no answer. Padme peeled off to search the living room while dale took the bedrooms. Silence hung heavy over the whole compound and padme could only hear her heart beating heavily. Something was wrong. She could feel it in her bones.

"agent kaur! We have two men down, kitchen area. Repeat, two men down."

Fuck. Where the hell was chaley? She turned into the study and flicked the lights on.

She recoiled immediately. The furniture in the room had been pushed to the sides of the room, except for one chair in the middle of the room. Tied to it, bloodied and unconscious—padme hoped—was chaley. Padme darted to the young woman's side and felt for a pulse. Still alive—just. She saw the vicious stab wounds in the young woman's abdomen, and her heart ached for the sweet young assistant.

Padme drew her gun and fired two shots into the roof, causing plaster to drop down on them. Dale and the other agents burst into the room as padme untied chaley and picked her up. God, she was tiny, probably less than a hundred pounds. Dale took her from padme as padme saw a note had been placed under chaley's limp body.

"let's get her to a hospital now," she ordered, as outside she saw the helicopter carrying her love take off. Relieved, she followed dale out to the car and sat in the back, cradling chaley, who was coming around. Padme was focused on pressing her hands down on chaley's wounds to keep the blood loss to a minimum.

"chaley? That's right, sweetheart, stay with me. Keep breathing. We're getting you to a hospital right now, darling."

Chaley opened her eyes and looked up at padme. "pad?"

Padme smiled. "that's right, sweetie, we're taking you to get help."

"they told me it wasn't personal. Don't let them win, pad; don't let them hurt him ..."

Padme moaned as chaley's head fell back, and the girl went limp in her arms. "dale! Fucking step on it!"

Dale got them to an emergency room in record time, but it was too late. The emergency room doctor declared chaley dead on arrival. He was sympathetic, but matter of fact with padme and dale. "she didn't stand a chance, i'm afraid. Her abdominal artery was severed in multiple places. She simply bled out."

Padme felt hollow. Over the few weeks she'd known chaley, she had grown to like the young assistant very much—she didn't deserve to die like this. No one did.

"fuck," dale said, his face pale. "fuck." Padme followed him out the ambulance. Dale put his head in his hands and then screamed. "fuck!"

Padme sat down on one of the benches outside and felt herself grow numb. Chaley had been murdered, and their safehouse was blown. Enver had been spirited away and now she wondered if she could even trust the people who had taken him. She remembered the note under chaley's body and pulled it out of her pocket, wincing at the blood that soaked the paper. She smoothed it out and read it.

Dale rubbed his hands on his head. "so, they know where we were keeping enver. Someone must have blabbed. Who the hell else knew apart from a very few of us? They knew about the house!"

Padme looked up at him, her face pale as she held up the note. "and they know about me."

Dale took the note from her and padme watched as his eyes widened as he read the message on the paper.

NEXT TIME, we'll gut your pretty indian girlfriend.

CHAPTER FIVE

Padme sat in henry's office. It had been two days since the murder, two days since she'd seen or spoken to enver. After they had read the note, dale had pleaded with her to tell henry about the threat.

"you don't have to say anything about your relationship with enver. Just take this threat seriously. If what happened to chaley ever happened to you ... i could not live with it, pad. Neither could enver."

So, here she was, waiting for henry to tell her what her next steps were. She had decided she would tell him everything, take her punishment, and ask if she could be put with enver.

"well," henry came into the room, shutting the door behind him. "i guess we now have two people to protect. The threat on that note was very real, padme. The ingles won't think twice about killing you to get to enver toscano."

"how did they know about us? I mean, about dale and i being mr. Toscano's protection detail?"

Henry's face was stern. "we are looking into it. Believe me, when i find them ..." he sighed. "so, assuming that you don't want off this case, i propose we take you to the same safehouse as toscano. You'll keep your badge and gun, but for all intents and purposes, you'll be treated as a protected witness also."

Padme sighed. "the babysitter becomes the babysat."

Henry's mouth hitched up in a smile. "suck it up. Mr. Toscano's lawyer tells me he thinks his client will only be questioned for one more day. After that ..."

"after that, what? We just let him walk into a viper's nest? They will kill him on sight, whether he's testified or not. They can't stop that now, but freddy ingles won't just let it lie."

Henry sat back in his chair, studying her. "we've offered mr. Toscano permanent relocation in the witness protection program, but he says he doesn't want it. Rumor has it he's in love with a woman here in seattle. You know anything about that?"

Padme prayed she didn't flush as she kept a blank expression. "no, sir, the protectee hasn't mentioned anything."

Henry's eyes never left hers. "i only ask because i know you and mr. Toscano seem friendly."

Padme nodded. "i would say that, sir. Within the confines of our roles, of course."

"of course."

He didn't believe her, she could tell, but she was too deep in the lie now. Jesus, she really had laid it on the line for this man, hadn't she? "is mr. Toscano safe where he is?"

Henry nodded. "he is. We told him about his assistant, and he's obviously very upset. He asked if you or agent fortuna were hurt and we told him you were fine. So, what i think would be best is if you pack a bag and we relocate you to where mr. Toscano is. He obviously trusts you, padme, and in his position, that's not an easy thing to do."

"will dale come with me?"

Henry hesitated. "agent fortuna is being reassigned."

Padme was shocked. "why? He did nothing wrong."

"i know that, padme." Henry's voice was kind. "he asked to be reassigned. Said he felt guilty for not protecting you."

"no!" Padme was distressed. "i'm fine, nothing happened to me. Chief, please, don't punish him for nothing. It wasn't his job to protect me."

"calm down, agent. Go talk to him, but he seemed pretty set. If he changes his mind, of course, let me know."

Padme sought Dale out immediately. He was eating a bowl of ramen in the mess. She sat down opposite him and glared at him until he looked up. He gave a resigned sigh. "you heard."

"what the hell, dale?"

Dale glanced around the room, making sure they weren't overheard before leaning closer. "they know we're a team. Maybe, by being separate, i can throw them off the track."

Padme rocked back. "you are not putting yourself up as bait. No freaking way, dale. No. I'm not some fragile little woman you have to save, captain america."

Dale rolled his eyes. "putting aside the fact that i would take a bullet for you any day, pad, i'm not that much of a neanderthal. I'm talking about working together, playing cat and mouse with them until someone slips up. Then we've got them, even if we have to take them down one operative at a time."

"we do not know who we are dealing with, dale, or how many of them there are. And someone," she hissed, lowering her voice, "is on the inside. I know it."

"paranoia, much?"

"how the fuck else did they find the safehouse?" Padme felt tears in her eyes. "how else did they kill chaley?"

Dale studied her for a long time. "pad, do you think i ever want to see you like that? Do you honestly not know how much you mean to me?"

She looked up sharply, misunderstanding him, and he laughed. "slow your roll. I meant as a sister. A best friend."

Padme relaxed. "good. I love you too, daleywhaley."

"a hell-no to that nickname."

Padme grinned, the banter cheering her. "so, daleywhaley, what's the plan?"

Dale laughed, shaking his head. "pain-in-the-ass woman. Well, first thing, you do as henry is telling you and get your ass over to enver. He needs you right now—in every way." He waggled his eyebrows, but padme shook her head at him.

"i lied to henry, told him nothing is going on."

"well, it isn't, is it? Not during the investigation, anyway."

Padme blushed, and dale's eye widened. "you didn't?"

"once," she admitted, "when everyone was asleep."

Dale considered and smiled mischievously. "nicely done, kaur."

She giggled but told him to shut up. "i cannot believe i risked everything for a jump."

"except it was more than that, right?" His voice was soft now. "you've fallen for him."

Padme hesitated and then nodded. "maybe i should quit."

Dale made a siren sound. "emergency, call the sisterhood, emergency." His lame imitation of a robot made padme laugh, and soon they were both crying with laughter.

"you are such a loser," she said, wiping her eyes.

"yeah, but i'm your best loser," he said smugly, and she grinned.

"yeah, you are. Give me a high five."

ALL THE WAY to the safehouse, even through so many detours and diversions she lost count, padme practiced her 'greeting the protectee' speech.

Hello again, mr. Toscano. Good to see you safe and well.

Mr. Toscano, hello, good to see you.

God, enver, you're the fucking sexiest man on this planet, get your clothes off right now and put your huge cock inside me ...

HER LIPS TWITCHED WITH A GRIN. No, that last one really wouldn't be appropriate—despite it being ... true. Shit. She loved him. No, no that wasn't possible. She'd only known him for a month. But everything in her body said it was true. She loved enver toscano. She closed her eyes and pictured him now, his crooked smile that changed his face from manly to boyish. That dark beard, those green eyes, that golden tanned skin. The feel of his lips against hers, on her nipples, on her clit. Jesus. Stop, she told herself, but then she couldn't stop the memory of his huge hard cock plunging into her swollen and wet cunt over and over and over ...

When they arrived at the new safe house, padme kept all her feelings inside her as she nodded to the security guard. "mr. Toscano is in his study, agent. Far end of the corridor as you go in."

"thank you." She made to move then stopped herself. "is mr. Dedalus here, agent?"

"no, ma'am. Just mr. Toscano."

"thank you," she said again, and then, her heart in her mouth, she walked to the study and knocked.

"come in."

She opened the door and saw him. Dressed in a sweater and blue jeans, he looked up from behind the desk, and the smile that spread across his face made her knees weak. Without a word, he got up, and with two long strides, he took her in his arms and kissed her. Padme, lost in his embrace, heard him lock the door behind her. A beat, then they were tearing at each other's clothes, desperate to feel each other's skin.

Enver lifted her, and she wrapped her legs around his waist as he plunged into her, pushing her back against the wall as they fucked with a desperation that was new to their lovemaking. Padme was glad the wall was concrete and not wood as enver slammed his hips into her over and over, his cock reaming her into a delirious state of pleasure.

"i love you," she gasped, not caring if he got freaked out. "i love you so much, enver toscano ..."

"ti amo, ti amo, ti amo," he whispered with real feeling, with tears in his eyes. "i love you too, il mia amore."

He made her come again and again as they clawed and bit and sucked at each other's bodies. Nothing existed in the world for them at that moment, just the joining of their bodies, the gaze of their eyes. Enver laid her on the desk, stroking the length of her body from her throat, cupping her breasts, down to her belly. Then he dropped to his knees and buried his head between her legs, sucking and teasing at her clit until she was moaning and coming again.

They fell to the floor with their limbs entwined as they caught their breaths, kissing and listening for anyone who might be close. Grinning up at him, padme kissed her way down enver's body and took his already-hard cock into her mouth. She teased him, hollowing out her cheeks as she sucked at him, massaging his balls with her hand, hearing his groans and his whispered murmuring of her name over and over. He tried to draw out as he was close but she shook her head. He came in her mouth, padme hungrily swallowing his seed down.

"god, padme ... padme ... ti amo ..." enver stood up and lifted her into his arms, kissing her as his green eyes went soft with love. "when i heard those gunshots, i thought i'd lost you. I tried to get out of the helicopter, but they took off. I was screaming at them—i'm afraid i cursed them out."

Padme chuckled, smoothing his hair back from his face. "and i'm glad they ignored you." Her smile faded. "i'm sorry about chaley. Such a sweet girl."

Enver's eyes were full of pain, and he nodded. "and they would not let me see her, or call her parents." He set padme down on her feet, and they got dressed. "come sit with me, darling."

He unlocked the door in case anyone got suspicious and opened the window to let some fresh air in. He sat next to padme and took her hand. "i cannot imagine what it must have been like to find her like that."

Padme sighed. "yes, you can. The same people who killed max and julia murdered chaley."

"henry told me there was a note with chaley's body. What did it say?"

Padme felt cold inside. They hadn't told him about the threat to her. Good. Good, that was for the best. Because otherwise, he would send her away. "just making sure you got the message. Forensics took care of it. I really didn't read much of it."

Enver seemed happy about that. He wrapped his arms around her and kissed her. "i'm sorry you had to go through that. Mio dio. I am crazy for dragging you into this world. I am selfish."

Padme kissed his cheek. "you didn't drag me anywhere; i came willingly. It's you and me now, whether it's publicly known or not. I've said it before, and i mean it. I'd take a bullet for you."

"and i'm going to ask you to stop saying that because it makes me want to break down." But he said it with a smile on his face. He leaned his forehead against hers. "i don't think the fbi knows what to do with me. Once my testimony is over, i'm cut loose."

Padme shook her head. "no. Look, they're offering witness protection. Take it."

Enver's smile faded. "they won't let me see you again. That's not an option. It's not as if i haven't got the resources to disappear from public life on my own."

"but why should you have to?" Padme felt a little hysterical. "it isn't fair."

He swept his hand through her hair and held her face in his hands. "who said life had to be fair? As long as i have you, nothing else matters."

"you'll always have me."

"good."

There was a knock at the door and they moved apart, trying to look as casual as possible as one of the security guards, sean, came in.

"agent kaur, we haven't met. I'm sean gray, head of security here."

Padme stood and shook the man's hand. "good to meet you. We should sit down and discuss mr. Toscano's protection while he's here. I understand you've been working in shifts?"

Sean gray gave her a bemused look. "we should also discuss your protection, agent kaur."

Oh, damn it. Padme could feel enver's stare. "i'm good, as long as mr. Toscano is good."

Sean nodded. "that's fair enough, but we have specific orders to protect both of you because of the threats."

"someone threatened agent kaur?" Enver's voice was hard.

Padme glared at sean, who finally caught on. "it's standard procedure when a protectee's safehouse is compromised to then protect the lead agents." It was a weak lie, but padme was grateful for him trying.

Sean made his excuses, obviously embarrassed, and left

them alone. Padme could feel the weight of enver's stare as she turned to face him.

"cara mia," she saw him barely contain his anger, "we're going to sit down, and you're going to tell me exactly what the fuck is going on."

PADME LAY ON HER BACK, staring up at the ceiling. She'd escaped here after she and enver had their very first argument. Enver was furious that she'd lied about the threats to her safety. She'd shot back that she was a big girl and could look after herself. Enver had lost it then, and padme realized just how scared he was of losing her.

"do you know what they did to julia?" He had raged at her. "i do. I saw the photos. They gutted her, padme. They cut her baby from her and killed them both. In front of max. Look what they did to chaley. Do you think they won't do it to you? Mio dio, padme, mio dio ..."

Eventually, she had left him to fume and come to find a bedroom to lie down in. Should she have told him about the threats?

Probably. Padme sighed and grabbed her cell phone and dialed the number of the only person she could talk to about this.

"hey, cutie."

"hey, d. Can you talk?"

"sure." Dale sounded out of breath. "it'll give me an excuse to stop working out. How's the love nest?"

"not very loving. Enver found out about the note."

"uh oh. I assume he didn't take it well."

Padme sighed. "no, he freaked on me. We're taking some time out right now."

Dale was still catching his breath. "you can't really blame

him, after what's happened. Hell, i don't want anything to happen to you either. None of us do."

Padme was quiet for a moment. "he told me he loved me."

"well, now," dale's voice softened, "of course he does."

Padme felt tearful. "what a fucking mess this all is."

"yup, princess, it is. Have you discussed what you're going to do after his testimony ends?"

"he won't go into witness protection because of me. God, dale, if he gets killed because of me …"

"you see? Don't be too hard on him when you feel the same way. Do you love him?"

"very much."

"then go make up with him. We'll figure out what to do next. It's not like he doesn't have the money to disappear. The question is—do you want to disappear with him, give up everything you've worked for, all your friends, family?"

Padme let a few silent tears fall. "that's just it, dale … i don't know."

6

CHAPTER SIX

Later that night there was a soft knock at her door and enver came in. He sat down on her bed, gazing down at her with pain in his eyes. Padme half-smiled at him. Enver slid his hand under her t-shirt and stroked her belly, circling her navel with his thumb before pushing her t-shirt up over her head. Padme sat up and kissed him as he freed her breasts from her bra and caressed them. Slowly, they undressed each other, and then enver gathered her to him.

"ti amo," he murmured as his lips trailed across her neck. Padme wrapped her legs around his waist, feeling his diamond-hard cock nudge against her sex. Enver teased her with the tip of it before plunging it into her.

God, when they were like this, padme knew she would give up everything for this, for him. Their lovemaking became more intense, their eyes locked on each other as they fucked, their panting synchronized as his cock plowed ever deeper into her swollen, wet cunt. Padme moaned as it hit every one of the sensitive nerve endings inside her, his mouth finding hers as their pace quickened.

"my beautiful padme, my love, il mia amore ..." his low,

sensual voice made her skin vibrate with pleasure, and now his mouth was on her nipple, sucking, biting, teasing. Padme gasped through a shattering orgasm, her body shuddering and liquefying as she came. When she felt his cock jerking, pumping creamy cum deep into her belly, she tightened her legs around him, not wanting him to withdraw.

"can we stay like this forever?" She whispered, and enver nodded.

"we can, principessa, we absolutely can. But it would mean leaving everyone and everything you know. Can you do that, padme? Can you really do that?"

And right at that moment, padme knew she could. She wanted to be with enver—openly, freely, more than anything. Even if being with him meant giving everything up and living a life on the run from his enemies.

Enver kissed her as he tightened his grip on her. "cara mia, if i could keep you safe forever, i would do it."

"i feel the same. Look, if tomorrow is your last day of testimony, then we have to decide tonight what our next move will be." Padme rubbed her eyes. "i'll have to tell my bosses that i'm quitting ..." her voice trailed off as she considered the weight of that decision. She had been so focused on her career for the last few years, so convinced it was the path her life was supposed to take, that abandoning it now for a man seemed overwhelming.

No. Not for a man—for this man. This gorgeous, sexy, funny man who loved her. He was watching her closely, and padme smiled at him. "a new life," she said firmly. "with you. Whatever the situation. We can face it together."

"you're sure?"

"i've never been so sure of anything in my life."

He kissed her again and then they were making love again, not caring who heard them, secure in the knowledge that their love could overcome anything.

They had exhausted each other, making love until dawn and, wrapped in each other's arms, they slept finally. Both of them woke with a start as the door to the bedroom was flung open. Brian dedalus stared down at them, a sneer on his face.

"get dressed," he snapped, his face raking over padme's body, a thin sheet the only thing separating her naked skin from his slimy gaze. "we leave in thirty minutes." He narrowed his eyes at padme, and she flushed. With just a look, he made her feel like a whore. Asshole.

"remind me to fire his ass," enver said darkly before smiling down at her. "good morning, beautiful."

She kissed him. "good morning, handsome."

"come shower with me."

In the hot shower, they made love, enver lifting her easily and pressing her back against the cool tile as he thrust into her. Padme clung to him, his lips against hers, savoring every thrust of his huge cock into her cunt. They fit together so perfectly, and she loved the feeling of her nipples pressing against his chest, her belly against his. She tangled her fingers in his hair, pulling hard as she came, throwing her own head back and giving a long moan of release. Enver's lips were on her throat as he pumped his seed deep into her belly.

Dressing quickly, they were about to leave the bedroom when enver grabbed her hand. "before we go, i want to say to you—thank you. Thank you for making my life something i want to keep living, with you. You have made me excited about the future. I was so down after max's death that i felt reckless, directionless. The moment i saw you at that party ... i love you so, so much, padme kaur. I can't wait to begin our life together."

a tear escaped her eye then. "oh god, enver ... you will never know how much you mean to me."

Their lips met in a passionate embrace. "i do know," enver said softly, "i see it in your eyes."

"i love you."

"ti amo, padme kaur. Ti amo."

THE JOURNEY to the court was thankfully uneventful, but padme was aware of brian dedalus glowering at her. She stared back at him, challenging him to say something about her and enver's relationship, but the lawyer merely smirked and looked away.

Enver took her hand as they walked down to meet henry jones and the rest of the fbi agents. Padme hesitated, but enver smiled down at her. "i'm not hiding anymore."

Padme nodded, winding her fingers through his. Dedalus would no doubt tell everyone, so why should they hide it anymore?

Henry's expression when he saw their linked hands went from surprise to resignation to disapproval. Sensing the shift in his emotions, padme excused herself from enver for a moment and drew henry to one side. "henry, i'm sorry. My mind is made up."

Henry shook his head, sighing. "i can't pretend i'm happy, padme. I championed you from the start, stuck my neck out for you, and you're throwing it away."

"for the best reason, henry. For the only reason. I'm in love with enver toscano."

Henry's eyes were troubled. "i don't think you have any idea what you're getting into. They will never stop hunting you."

Padme nodded. "i know. But he means everything to me. We'll handle whatever comes, together."

Henry sighed. "if that's the way you want it to be, agent kaur, i'm going to have to relieve you of duty. Your badge and gun."

Padme handed them to him. "thank you for everything, henry."

Henry leaned closer. "please, pad, change your mind. Don't make me fire you."

Padme kissed his cheek. "you don't need to fire me, henry. I quit."

"think about what you're doing."

"i have," she said, meeting his gaze. "i know what my life is meant to be now."

She made her way back to enver, showing him her empty gun holster. "so, i'm just here as your lover now, baby. I can come into the courtroom, support you."

He squeezed her hand, dipping his head to kiss her. "you are my world."

"glad to hear it." Brian dedalus came up behind them. "because i've just put in a formal complaint about you, agent kaur. I'm sure your bosses will be displeased with your behavior."

Enver opened his mouth to speak, but padme shook her head. "no, please, let me." She turned to look at brian. "fuck off, dedalus, you slimy-faced-patrick-bateman-wannabe. If you're trying to get me fired, it's too late. I already quit. Enver and i have been together since before i ever met you, so mind your own business, would you please? Jackass."

She turned her back on the lawyer. Enver was having trouble hiding his smirk.

"fucking little whore," brian hissed, apoplectic, and spat at her. His saliva hit her in the face, and an incensed enver lunged for brian.

"stop, stop!" Padme got between them, wiping her face. "brian, walk away right now. Enver, they're calling you."

Enver let go of brian, who then dusted himself off. "dedalus, the second this is over, you're fired. Get out of my sight."

Brian gave a strange smirk of triumph but said nothing more, stalking off. Padme breathed out, relaxing as enver took her hand. "ready, love?"

PADME WATCHED her lover as he calmly answered the questions the prosecution and defense were putting to him. She looked at the defendants, lower-ranking members of frederick ingles' organization. All this for them, she said to herself. Was it worth it?

As enver was released from the custody box, it seemed so anti-climactic, but his smile when he rejoined her made her heart swell.

"we're free," he said. "now, let's disappear."

He kissed her as she led him from the courtroom. She saw brian dedalus in front of them. He turned as they reached the stairs.

To padme's horror, at the last moment, she saw the gun in brian's hand. He leveled it at enver, and it all happened in a second. Padme threw herself in front of enver, pushing him down as brian fired the gun and she felt hot metal slam into her belly.

"fucking bitch!" Daedalus' shirt exploded with red as the other agents took him down, but he managed to get off another shot, this time aiming for padme deliberately. The bullet ripped into her stomach. Adrenaline flooded her body, and she was more concerned with enver than herself.

He was underneath her as padme flipped over to check enver wasn't shot. There was so much blood. "are you hit? Are you hit?" She was frantic now, her hands roaming his body searching for wounds. Enver's eyes were huge, full of pain. He shook his head.

"no, baby, it's not my blood. It's not my blood. Oh god, padme

... someone help her, please. He shot her ..." he was screaming now as padme realized that her whole body was on fire and that the blood soaking them both was her own.

Someone pushed her aside and grabbed enver, yanking him up as he screamed for someone to help her. Padme lay on her back, barely able to breathe as she watched enver, still shouting with his eyes fixed on her, reaching out his arms toward her as he was being dragged away by his protection.

"i love you," she whispered as the darkness flooded her vision ...

CHAPTER SEVEN

Six months later ...

HENRY JONES SIGHED as the field office receptionist nodded towards his visitor. "padme, this has to stop."

Padme struggled to her feet, the cane she was using helping her up. Since being shot, she had gone through long and extensive—and painful—rehab, but her progress was slowed by the fact that every day, she came here, to her old workplace to ask henry one question.

Where is enver?

Padme, her lovely face pale, fixed henry with a determined look. "henry, i'm going to keep coming here until you help me. Where is enver?"

Henry shook his head but said nothing, instead helping her towards his office. When she was settled in the chair, he sat back down opposite her, studying the young woman who had thrown everything away for the man she loved. "pad, i've told you again and again. Enver toscano took himself out of protective custody and disappeared."

"if that were true, he would have come for me."

Henry sighed again. "so, you've told me over and over. Look, sweetheart." He leaned forward, giving her a warm smile. "enver is wherever he is, and the fact he hasn't come for you ... doesn't that say it all? Pad, you gave up everything you had for him, and you still got shot, and even after that, he left you."

Padme fixed him with a glare. "if he didn't care, why did he pay for all my medical costs? Why are there hundreds of millions of dollars in my checking account? I haven't touched any of it because if i do, i'll be admitting he's gone. If he isn't contacting me, it's because he can't, and that means he's dead." She choked over the words. "or frederick ingles has him."

"or maybe it was enver's way of saying goodbye?" Henry's words were soft, but padme looked away from his gaze.

"no. He loves me."

"sometimes i forget how young you are." Henry rubbed his hands over his head. "i never thought you were the type of woman who would abandon everything for the sake of some good sex and a handsome face."

Padme rocked back. "it's more than that between enver and i, and i don't appreciate being patronized. I haven't abandoned anything. I made an informed decision when i quit."

"but you didn't tell severin or any of your friends that you were planning to disappear from their lives entirely."

Padme was silent for a moment before she got up. "i'll come again tomorrow. If you don't help me, i'll find a way to find enver. He's out there, and god knows what is happening to him. He put his neck on the line to help bring down the ingles, and the fbi just abandoned him."

She limped out of the door, with henry staring unhappily

after her. He closed his eyes and thought for a long moment, before picking up his phone. "it's me. I need to call in a favor."

Padme saw dale waiting outside her apartment and felt a wave of annoyance. He helped her from the cab. "did you get sent?" She asked, not caring if she sounded pissed. She was pissed.

Dale, used to her moods by now, shrugged. "henry's concerned, like the rest of us."

Padme let him help her inside her apartment. "how about i make us some coffee?" Dale said, making sure she was comfortable. As the coffee brewed, he studied her. "you don't look so good, pad. You sleeping?"

Padme shook her head. She felt exhausted now, drained, and worst of all, heartbroken. Tears came easily, and they did now.

"oh, pad." Dale's arms were around her then, comforting her, and she let a few more tears escape.

"i miss him. I just miss him." She started to cry in earnest now. Dale let her cry herself out.

"sweets, i know you don't want to hear this, but you need to move on now. Come on, i don't have to tell you this."

Padme sat up, drying her eyes with the palms of her hand. "fuck, dale, i don't know how my life has turned out like this. I really don't." She moved and winced, and dale frowned.

"you still in pain?"

She nodded. "docs think it's psychosomatic, but i swear they left something in there."

"like what?"

She gave him a grin. "branding iron, from the burn of it."

"hair straighteners."

"bonfire."

"ouch." But dale grinned at her, obviously glad to see her

joking after her distress. Padme sighed and leaned her head back on the couch.

"so, no job, no lover. Wow. I could write a book on fucking up, couldn't i?"

"what did you fuck up? You fell in love, is all. You did nothing wrong—in fact, you did everything right. Even after you quit, you still saved the protectee."

Padme stared at him. "then why did he leave me?"

"maybe he figured he was bad news. You got shot because of him."

"i got shot because brian dedalus was working for frederick ingles."

"we don't know that. For all we know, dedalus could have just been jealous of you and enver. Maybe he was in love with one of you and couldn't live with it. He must have known we'd take him down once he started shooting."

"asshole."

Dale nodded. "right. So, working for frederick ingles … i don't know."

Padme looked at him unhappily. "what if he's killed enver, dale? I have to know." She hesitated. "will you help me? Please?"

She'd asked before, of course, but now she felt dale was listening, really listening to her. And yes, she needed to know whether her lover was alive or not. She couldn't move on until she knew. If he were alive and didn't want her—yes, it would hurt like hell, but she would have some closure, at least. Dale let out a long breath.

"i won't do anything to risk my job at the bureau, but within those conditions … yes, all right. I'll give you three months, pad, and then we call it quits, and you move on with your life. Spend some of that money on yourself."

She half-smiled at him. "it's not my money. But as for the rest, okay. Thank you. Three months."

Three months to find out whether the love of her life was dead or alive …

And whether he still wanted her.

Padme went to bed that night a little lighter at heart. Since that terrible day in the courtroom, it had felt like her heart had been the one to take those three bullets. When she awoke in the hospital three days after the shooting, barely able to move and in incredible pain, her first question had been: "is enver okay?"

Her pseudo-mother severin had stroked the hair back from padme's forehead and told her that enver hadn't been hurt but that they'd had to take him into protective custody. Padme had been relieved, and as she'd recovered, it had given her strength to know that soon, she and enver would be reunited.

But it hadn't worked that way. One day, henry had come to visit her and told her that enver had gone. "we don't know where, sweetheart."

"bullshit. He wouldn't just leave me. Is this some plan you dreamed up to protect me?"

She wouldn't listen to henry's explanations of why enver hadn't been allowed to contact her. It was only when it came time for her to settle her medical expenses that she discovered they had all been covered by enver. On top of that, her bank had called her about the large deposit that had been made into her checking account.

"excuse me? How much did you say?" She couldn't believe this wasn't a prank.

"over seven hundred million dollars, ms. Kaur. Obviously, we're calling to set a meeting to discuss investing the sum and …"

"this is a joke, right? Dale? Is this you?"

It had taken some persuasion and a quick login onto her

online banking account to see the numbers in black and white before she believed it.

Credit $735,589,60.00
　Creditor e. Long.

'E. Long'. Eddie long—the name enver had used to check into the hotel where they had spent that incredible erotic weekend. Enver had given her almost a billion dollars? She had gone through many emotions, the overriding one being that she didn't want his money and he must have known that. Was this a kiss off? If it was, it was a humiliating one and completely out of character for enver.

Padme rolled onto her back now and stared up at the ceiling. No. Something else was going on and she couldn't for the life of her figure out what it was.

"if you're out there, baby," she whispered, "please. Come find me."

She heard footsteps on the balcony outside her bedroom window. Another of enver's mysterious gifts had been to hire around-the-clock-security. She was still on frederick ingles' radar, it would seem. She hadn't heard or witnessed anything suspicious since the shooting, but it never hurt to be cautious. Maybe it's because enver is dead and he has no more need for revenge.

She squeezed her eyes shut. No. No, i won't believe that until they show me his body.

She rolled onto her side and curled up as comfortably as she could. Despite what she'd told dale, the pain inside had been getting worse, not better, and her doctors were worried. Her spine had been damaged by the bullets smashing through her soft abdomen, and now it was constantly inflamed. She'd had steroid injections and god knows what else but padme knew—she would probably never regain full function of her own body.

Stop dwelling on it. Remember something good, something happy ... try as she might, she could now only equate happiness with her time with enver. That first weekend, that incredible, life-changing weekend ...

IT WAS SATURDAY NIGHT. They had spent the day making love, ordering room service, and now they were soaking in the large tub, padma's head resting back on his shoulder. She looked around at him, and he pressed his lips to hers.

"have i told you today how beautiful you are?" She felt the vibration of his deep voice through his chest and smiled at him.

"as long as you think so." She turned around in the tub, straddling him, running her hands over the firm planes of his chest. She didn't think she could ever get over the way her heart fluttered at a single look at his face. He looked so boyish and fun one moment, then serious and almost dangerous the next. He gazed back at her with clear green eyes rimmed by the thickest, darkest lashes she'd ever seen.

"i think you're the beautiful one," she whispered.

Enver's hand reached up to cup the back of her neck as he pulled her to him, crushing his lips against hers. He kissed her slowly, his tongue delving deep into her mouth, massaging, caressing hers. His free hand moved in a gentle pattern on her belly, making it quiver with longing before his hand moved down to caress her clit.

Padme moaned with pleasure as his fingers twisted and rubbed at her. She gasped as he slid two fingers and then three fingers inside her. "i can feel your heartbeat through the walls of your cunt," he said softly, his eyes never leaving hers. "god, i want to fuck you forever, feel your thighs clamp around my waist, feel your belly against mine, your breasts pressed against my chest, your lips on mine." He fisted her long dark hair at the nape of her neck, his gaze intense now. "can you feel how hard i am for you, principessa?"

She slid her hand down to his cock, so huge and diamond-hard in her hands, and she smiled at him. "put that inside me," she whispered, and with one easy movement, he lifted her and impaled her onto him. Padme shivered with pleasure as his cock filled her and she began to ride him slowly, never losing eye contact. "baby?"

Enver smiled at her. "yes, my darling one?"

"i have noticed, in between the times you are playing around, you look kind of ... dangerous. I like it."

He raised his eyebrows. "you do?"

"i do. So, i'm saying, if there's anything you want me to do ... to be yours, i would do it." Padme was blushing furiously, but the thought of him getting masterful with her was really turning her on. Enver got it and grinned.

"a little roleplay?"

Padme chuckled, reaching down so she could massage his balls while she fucked him. "anything."

"well then, let me think ... the idea of you tied up and helpless—i mean, in this situation –while i fuck you sounds good to me." His eyes suddenly lit up. "or, maybe even ..."

He trailed off, and in frustration, padme gave his balls a squeeze. He winced, then laughed at her sulky face. "so impatient. Well, okay then ... how would you like it if we almost got caught while we fucked?"

Padme smiled slowly. "that would be pretty thrilling. And it would remind me of our first tryst. I like that."

"indeed. But what i'm talking about is actually fucking in a crowd of people, not behind closed doors, actually in the same room."

"hmm, that sounds intriguing, but how would it work in reality?"

"you'd have to wear a short skirt and no underwear," he said matter-of-factly, and she couldn't help laugh at the expression on his face.

"and you'd have to fuck me from behind, i'm guessing."

"and you'd have to make sure you give nothing away with your facial expression. Do you think you'd be able to manage that?"

Padme laughed. "that is the only problem." She thrust her hips hard, and enver groaned. "see? When your cock is inside me, all i do is gasp and moan and scream your name … danilo."

There was a strange expression in his eyes, and she smiled at him. "i'd much rather be shouting your real name."

He nodded. "same here, penny."

They both laughed softly. "well, if we're going to be other people, then i say we take that into consideration. Let's play 'we never met before.'"

Enver's lips twitched in amusement. "so, again, much like how we met."

"well," padme considered. "you didn't fuck me in public, and i remember wearing underwear, because you ripped it off of me."

"so, i did." Enver looked very pleased with himself, and padme laughed and tried to look disapproving. "they were my favorite pair."

"i'll buy you more."

"and i'm still wondering what harpa will think when she finds an abandoned pair of panties on her office floor."

"she won't. They're in the pocket of my pants. I have ocd when it comes to underwear."

"or you just collect ladies' used underwear, you perv." Padme grinned as he threw his head back and laughed. He was so easy to be with, to tease. She'd never have been able to have a silly conversation like this with any of her past lovers—especially not while their cock was still inside her. Enver put his hand on his heart and feigned seriousness.

"just yours, i swear."

"glad to hear it." She increased her pace, ramming her hips against him and taking him in deeper and deeper until neither could talk. They were both panting as they came, enver pulling her to him and kissing her as she gasped with pleasure.

Two hours later, they caught a cab into seattle's nightclub area and randomly chose a club to go to. Inside, the heat and sweaty atmosphere added to their fun, as well as the quadruple tequila shots enver ordered for them. Padme pulled a face as she downed it. "so gross."

Enver laughed "then why did you drink it?"

"courage," she said as she started to dance around him, making him laugh. He ran his hands down her body.

"you don't need courage," he said, pulling her to him, "you're the most beautiful, sexy, gorgeous woman in this room. In this city." He kissed her until her head spun, then nuzzled her nose. "in this world, cara mia."

God, he was intoxicating. She kissed him, then moved her lips to his ear. "fuck me. Fuck me hard."

They danced together as the music got slower and more sensual, the people around them locked into their own sensual foreplay. Enver danced her to the far wall then whispered, "turn around, baby, face away from me."

Padme did as she was told, grinding her ass into his groin, hearing his low chuckle. She was wet already at the thought of him being inside her again. He lifted the back of her short, dark red dress and pulled her back into him. Padme leaned her head back on his shoulder, and he kissed her to muffle her cry as he wrapped his arms around her and thrust into her.

Padme continued to sway as enver fucked her, timing his thrusts to the rhythm of the music. Padme was lost in a delirium of pleasure—this man had complete dominion over her body, his hand splayed on her belly, his lips against her neck. Fucking openly in front of these people was the hottest thing she'd ever done. Padme didn't care if they were found out, and as she shuddered through an orgasm, felt him come and heard his groan.

"cara mia, cara mia …"

When they had recovered themselves and checked to make sure no security guards were heading their way to kick them out after their little show, padme turned and kissed him with every inch of passion she felt for him. "danilo, whatever your name is, you are the most amazing man i've ever met. If we never see each other again, i will always remember this night."

His green eyes crinkled and he leaned his forehead against his. "i cannot imagine, principessa, that we will ever not be in each other's lives now. In fact, i promise you, here and now, that for as long as you want me, i will be with you."

PADME GROANED, now, feeling the ghostly strength of his arms around her, his soft lips against hers. "you lied," she whispered. "i loved you, and you lied. Where are you now, enver? Where are you?"

CHAPTER EIGHT

Padme stacked the books up on the cart and pushed them to the far end of the bookstore. She'd been hired on by the kind and sweet owner, beth, as a favor. "for as long as you need, honey," the older woman said.

Beth was a friend of severin's, so padme knew her mother had something to do with her getting this job. The short hours suited her just fine—she still couldn't stand up for long periods, but the sedate quietude of the place relaxed her. Lately, beth had given her more responsibility, and it was the perfect thing to help distract her from the rest of her life's problems for a couple hours a day. It was tempting to sit and read all day, as she had during her recovery—that way she could focus on the story rather than obsess over enver.

She had finally stopped going to henry. She knew it was pointless and with dale helping her, she felt like she was doing something. But they hadn't made any headway—enver was still lost in the wind.

"excuse me?"

Padme turned to see a tall man, good-looking, impeccably dressed standing behind her.

"can i help you?" She forced a smile onto her face.

He smiled down at her, almost arrogantly, and padme felt her skin prickle with irritation.

"i hope you can, padme. Hello." He held out his hand to her. "i'm frederick ingles."

CHAPTER NINE

Padme felt the blood in her veins turn to ice. She shot a panicked look at beth, who was talking to another customer at the front of the store. She looked back at ingles. "if you're going to kill me, take me somewhere else and do it. Don't hurt anyone else, please. I'll come with you, i won't make a fuss."

Frederick ingles threw his head back and laughed loudly, garnering the attention of everyone in the bookstore. Padme could feel the panic rising in her throat.

"please." She hissed at him, but he shook his head.

"why on earth would i kill you, my dear padme? You misunderstand my visit. I merely came to ask you if you would be so kind as to join me for lunch. We can take a cab or even walk to the small coffeehouse down the block if you feel uncomfortable. I simply want to talk to you."

Padme shot beth another look, but her boss was still chatting away happily. She looked back at the man in front of her.

"fine. I get off in ten minutes. Wait at the coffeehouse. I'll be there."

Frederick smiled but it did not reach his eyes. "make sure

you're there, padme." He reached out and stroked a finger down her cheek. "so beautiful. I can see why he loved you."

Loved. God, the pain was almost overwhelming. Padme watched frederick ingles walk out of the store and head down to the coffeeshop. What the hell did he want? To torment her before he killed her? To tell her enver was dead?

Bastard. Padme pulled her cell phone from her pocket and called dale. He warned her against keeping the meeting. "please, pad, don't go."

"i have to," she said. "i'm scared he'll do something to someone i love."

She heard dale hiss down the phone in frustration. "god, pad. Look, i'm coming by. Don't worry, i won't make myself obvious unless you need me. I'll check out who he's got watching you."

Padme felt her shoulders slump in relief. "thanks, d, i appreciate it."

TEN MINUTES LATER, she said goodbye to beth and walked slowly to the coffeehouse, her heart thumping. She saw him sitting at a table outside and cautiously approached him. Frederick ingles looked up and smiled, rising to draw out a chair for her.

"thank you," she said stiffly, leaning her cane against the table. Frederick frowned at it.

"you are still in pain from the shooting."

She nodded. "yes, from when i was shot by your stooge."

Frederick gave her a half-smile. "brian dedalus did not work for me, padme. I did not order your shooting."

"just enver's?"

"no. I would not have been stupid enough to pull a stunt like that. And if i had wanted you dead, beautiful one, i would have done it myself."

He met her gaze with dead eyes, and she shivered. This man was a true psychopath. "what about chaley? Why did you kill her?"

Frederick shrugged. "to send a message. And, of course, because it was fun."

Anger flashed through her. "you bastard. She was only a kid, and you butchered her for fun? What the fuck is wrong with you?"

"my dear padme, under the table, i have a .22 with a silencer in my left hand, and it is aimed at your belly right now. So, i wouldn't try to make me angry, if i were you. I would hate to add to your pain." Frederick gave her the smile of a besotted lover.

He is insane. Padme closed her eyes and drew in a deep breath. "what do you want from me, ingles? If you've come to ask me where enver is, you're out of luck. I don't know. I've been trying to find him for six months."

"ah, but you don't have the resources i do. No, padme, i just want to know about every single second you spent in toscano's company. Every single detail," he leered now. "even down to how he fucked you, how his cock felt in your cunt ..."

"stop." Padme felt sick, but she raised her chin and stared back at him. "and if i don't tell you?"

"then there will be a bullet for every single person you know and love. Your friend severin; i hear she is the woman you consider your mother. The chef, harpa ... both her and her lovely sister, and their husbands. Your friends at the fbi. Your partner. And then, of course, you, my beautiful padme. No quick bullet for you, but a long, slow death at the end of my knife."

Padme felt as if she were having an out-of-body experience. "why haven't you killed me yet?"

"because i want toscano." Frederick dropped all pretense of friendliness. "make no mistake, ms. Kaur, when i find him, i will end him. And then i will come back for you. It's simple. The more you tell me, the longer you live."

"but you'll kill me anyway."

"yes. Like i said, it'll be fun." He drained his coffee and stood, and she saw him tuck his weapon back into his waistband. He was elegantly dressed, expensively, too. If you saw him, you might even think he was handsome and desirable, padme thought, but underneath that mask, he is pure evil. He looked down at her, then suddenly bent his head and kissed her roughly on the mouth. She jerked away from him, sickened.

Ingles laughed. "yes, it will be fun, darling one. I might even fuck you before i kill you. I'll be in touch."

And he was gone.

Padme was trembling violently, unable to move from her seat. She wanted to scream and cry at the humiliation of it all, the horror, but she was frozen. She felt arms wrap around her and dale's warm, comforting presence. "come on, sweetheart. I'm going to take you home now."

SHE COULDN'T REMEMBER the journey back to her apartment. Dale tucked her into the couch, then brought a blanket to wrap around her. Making her some hot tea, he waited while she told him everything ingles had said to her. Dale stood, angry, and paced the room.

"fucker. Cocksucking motherfucker," he said, and padme nodded.

"he exudes evil," she said softly. "i've been around some bad people, but nothing like him. He's not even human."

Dale sat next to her, putting his arm around her shoulders. "i won't let him hurt you."

But padme was beyond being comforted. Enver was gone.

The only positive thing was that ingles had confirmed he was still alive. Except ...

That meant enver was alive and didn't want her. She felt sick.

"maybe you should use that money enver left you and disappear."

Padme looked up at dale. "but i can't hide severin, or harpa, or any of you away. Why should you all have to leave your lives for this asshole?"

Dale hissed in frustration. "fuck."

Padme sighed and leaned against him. "i have no idea what to do now, dale. None."

And he didn't have an answer for her.

FREDERICK INGLES WENT BACK to his hotel and waved his assistant away. He wanted to be alone now, to savor his conversation with padme kaur. Christ, she was one of the most beautiful women he had ever met, and his bloodlust was as rampant as his cock, his hard-on pressing tightly against his pants.

He stripped and went to the shower, fisting the root of his cock, then as the hot water sprayed down on him, he masturbated, thinking of her creamy dusky skin, her large brown eyes, her full breasts. He had to admit it—enver toscano had good taste. He, frederick, would sample what she had to offer before he killed her. As he came, he wondered if he should keep her alive, keep her with him as his toy. He could always end her if he grew tired of her. He knew she wouldn't come willingly—that just made it sound more appealing.

Frederick came hard, shooting his seed into the drain and grunting. Yes, he decided, panting for air, he would make padme kaur his own personal sex toy.

It would make her eventual murder more ... Fun.

. . .

ONE WEEK LATER, and padme hadn't heard anything from ingles. She was cooking a late supper for severin, who sat at her kitchen counter watching her adoptive daughter. Severin was watching padme as she moved with obvious pain around her small kitchen.

"girl, sit down before you fall down. Here, let momma do that." She took the pan of pasta from padme and dumped the contents into the strainer. Padme perched on the stool gratefully, rubbing her right leg.

"it is getting better, mom. The physio told me today i was making great progress."

"physically, maybe, but mentally ... don't give me that look, young lady, i can see it in your eyes."

Padme shrugged and looked away from the mother's penetrating gaze. She could never hide things for long from severin—although she had kept frederick ingles' threats to herself. I'm going to be murdered soon. Every day since the meeting, she said those incredulous words to herself. She still couldn't believe this was her life: the love of her life gone and a psychopath calmly telling her she was going to die violently.

Severin had divided the pasta into bowls and handed one to padme. "eat all of that, padme. You need to put on some weight."

Padme had no appetite at first, but as soon as she bit down on the first piece, she realized she was ravenous. She finished her pasta and went back for seconds, much to severin's approval. Padme snagged a carton of orange juice from the fridge, offering some to severin, who shook her head.

"no, thanks, darling. Now, after you finish that, i'm going to do the dishes. You go sit in the living room. I'll be there in a moment."

Padme did as she was told and curled into the couch. The pasta carbs were making her feel so tired, and she closed her eyes. So tired ... so tired ...

. . .

"PADME. PADME. PADME, OPEN YOUR EYES."

God, leave me alone, i just want to sleep.

"padme, i know you're waking up. Open your eyes, please."

The voice was unfamiliar. Padme frowned and opened her eyes. Her throat was sore, painful, and now she could see she was in the emergency room. Severin, her usually stoic face wracked with despair and tear-stained, stood by her bed. She clutched at padme's hand as she gazed at her adoptive daughter

"darling? Oh, thank god."

"what's going on?" Padme managed to croak before a fit of coughing took her voice. Severin looked at the doctor, who nodded, then she helped padme sip some cold water. Padme drank, feeling immediate relief. "why am i here?"

The doctor and severin exchanged a glance. "sweetheart," her mother said, "they had to pump your stomach. Darling ... why did you take all those pills? Why ...?" She broke off, distressed, and padme reached for her.

"mom, i never took any pills. What are you talking about?"

"i couldn't wake you. They had to pump your stomach, but you had already digested them. You've been out for a long time."

Padme frowned, trying to remember if she had accidentally taken too many of her pain killers. "i don't remember doing that."

The doctor cleared his throat. "we don't know if it was pills, actually. Whatever it is you took, it was enough to knock you out. We won't know what until the blood tests come back, but there doesn't appear to be any liver or kidney damage. Your throat will be sore for a time. I apologize for that."

Padme gave him a half-smile. "i forgive you. After all, you were trying to save my life."

When they were alone, severin let her anger show. "how dare you try and kill yourself?"

"i swear i didn't, mom," padme shook her head. "i wouldn't do that."

Severin's body slumped. "i know, darling. I'm just so confused. I know you've been in a lot of pain, and with enver being gone ... for a moment, i thought you'd reached rock bottom."

Padme squeezed her hand. "no, i think rock bottom is still coming, but i'm not there yet."

She grinned to show severin she was joking. Severin's smile was grim. "just don't give up, is all i ask."

Padme leaned her head against her mother's shoulders. "never."

SEVERIN HAD FALLEN asleep in the chair next to padme's bed when the doctor came back to see them. "no pills," he said, in a grim voice. "i'm afraid to say that it seems you were drugged with a date rape drug."

Padme gaped at him. "what? How?"

"no idea."

Padme frowned, trying to recall when she had been in another person's company. "how quickly do they work?"

"pretty quickly. Within a half hour, i would say. Your dose was mild enough not to do any damage, but strong enough to knock you out. I'd prefer you stay here overnight just to be sure, but i think you may be able to go home in the morning."

Padme thanked him. After he'd left, padme tried to remember what she had eaten or drunk with severin that night. She knew it couldn't have been severin who drugged her. Everything she had, severin had also eaten or drunk ... apart from the orange juice.

Padme snagged severin's cell phone from her purse and called dale. She explained where she was and why. "dale, could you go to my apartment and grab that oj? Have it tested for drugs."

"you think someone got in?"

"i do, although i'm not sure why. Maybe they wanted me out of action so they could snatch me. I don't know."

"i'll get on it."

Padme smiled down the phone. "thanks, d, you're the best. Oh, hey," a thought suddenly struck her, "would you have the place scanned for cameras or bugs? It just occurred to me that ingles might have rigged my apartment."

"will do. You just get some rest. Love you."

"love you too, daleywhaley."

He laughed. "that sounds more like the old you. Later."

Padme ended the call and smiled to herself. Weirdly, she felt more energized than she had for a while. Probably because of the extra sleep, she told herself. She just didn't understand why someone would go to the trouble of drugging her—and then not do anything.

One of the night nurses came in, struggling under the weight of a huge bunch of flowers. "didn't even know they did deliveries this late. Here you go, hun." She handed padme an envelope.

"thank you. Gosh, they're gorgeous." Padme was astonished at the beautiful bouquet— all bright jewel tones. She opened the envelope and pulled out ... a lotto ticket. A washington state hit 5 lottery ticket. What the hell?

She turned over and saw a signature on the back of it – e. Latimer.

E. Latimer? What the hell is going on?

She looked for any other identifying marks, but there were none. She read the numbers to herself.

0/2/78/23/0

What was wrong with this picture? She read the numbers again before it dawned on her—the lotto didn't go up to seventy-eight, and there were definitely no zeros. It wasn't a real ticket. Someone was trying to tell her something.

Enver?

"what is it?" She hissed softly to herself, racking her brain. But try as she might, she could not make a connection.

It was just after four a.m. And the hospital was silent, only the soft beep of machinery making any noise when padme awoke, gasping, not from pain, but from realization.

Eddie long. E. Latimer. The strange and huge sum of money transferred to her checking account, almost but not quite seven hundred and fifty million. The weirdly ordered numbers on the lotto ticket.

They were longitude and latitude.

Enver was telling her where to find him.

10

CHAPTER TEN

Dale was waiting at her apartment when padme got home. Severin kissed her daughter goodbye and hugged dale. "look after her," she said with a twinkle in her eye. She had always liked dale. If padme and dale had suddenly decided they were in love, severin would have thrown a party.

Padme smiled at dale as he studied her. "you okay, sweets?"

She nodded. "i really, really am. I got my fight back."

He squinted at her. "you got drugged ... and it's a good thing?"

"i think i was meant to go to the hospital. I got some flowers there." She stopped and looked around. "is it safe to talk here?"

Dale nodded and grinned. "oh, yes."

"no bugs?"

"no, there were. Or rather, there's one camera, but somehow i don't think you'll be mad about it."

"about someone spying on me? I think i might be," padme said grimly, ready to throw a fit and start yelling. Dale, chuckling, held his hands up.

"slow your roll and listen to me. There's one camera, in this room only. Look up at the top shelf. Notice anything?"

Padme looked up at her shelf. "no." She blinked in confusion.

Dale sighed, amused. "i forget that you're about as domesticated as angelina jolie. Look again. See the dust on the books? Okay. See the one book that has no dust on it?"

Padme squinted at it and started laughing. "the story of o? Are you kidding me?"

Dale smiled. "the person who's watching you probably hopes you've read that cover-to-cover."

Padme's hand was at her mouth. "enver?" She whispered it, and dale nodded.

"when i found it, i was about to disable it, but then i got a phone call."

"from him?" Padme's heart was pounding painfully hard.

Dale shook his head. "from a woman. She asked me not to remove the camera, that it was, how did she put it—a link that her employer wanted. I asked her why the hell i shouldn't rip the damn thing out and told her that her employer could go fuck himself. I was sure she worked for ingles. I was about to hang up when she said something to me. She said 'lemon. Left inner thigh.'"

"oh my god." Padme's legs wobbled and she sat down. "my tattoo. There are only four people in the world who know i have that. Me, the tattooist, you, and enver. Well, maybe the people at the emergency room by now. But how would this woman know? It has to be enver."

Dale nodded and sat opposite her. "i think so, too. So, i left the camera where it was and thought i'd tell you."

Padme put her face in her hand and gave a sob, just one, but then looked up smiling. She went to the bookcase and stared up at the camera. "has it got a microphone? Can he hear me?"

"i think so. I think he heard me cussing when i found it and he called whoever that woman was to stop me."

Padme chuckled and looked back at the camera. "i love you," she said, and smiled. "and ... i know."

She blew a kiss at the camera.

"sappy."

She laughed and flicked a pillow at dale. "shut up. Listen, i have something to tell you, but i have to be certain no one will overhear us. Let's go outside. Leave your cell phone in here."

Dale's eyebrows shot up. "really?"

Padme nodded, her smile grim. "oh, yes. Really."

DALE: rule one. Don't use your phone or your computer. Don't go to an internet café or use a friend's computer or phone. You don't know where ingles has eyes.

PADME HANDED the stranger's phone back to her with a smile. "thank you so much. My husband is on his way. Can i pay you for the time?"

"oh no, no, it's fine. Take care." The woman waved and smiled her goodbye, and padme grinned.

No husband was on his way. She had to admit, she'd faked the phone call perfectly. It had taken only a minute to punch in the two strings of numbers she'd memorized.

Latitude 0.278230 longitude 73.432896

SHE FINALLY HAD A LOCATION. The island of gan, addu atoll, the maldives, indian ocean. Enver was in paradise.

. . .

DALE: rule two. When you find out where he is, do not say it aloud. To anyone. Not even yourself. Do not tell anyone, not even me. Find a way of communicating in silence to enver via the camera. Do not rush this—it's vital. Don't be tempted to run off to the nearest airport. Plan this. It's been six months; you can wait a little longer—you rush it now, you'll both end up dead.

"my, pad, you'll end up spending all your paycheck in here." Beth smiled at her as she packed another bag full of the books pad had just bought. "good choices, too, a lot of classics." She looked through the selection. "lolita. One of my favorites."

Padme smiled. "thought it was time i caught up on my reading. I have a lazy weekend planned with junk food and books."

Beth chuckled. "that sounds like heaven. Have a good couple of days, sweetheart."

"see you monday?"

"sure thing."

When padme exited the shop, frederick ingles was waiting outside.

DALE: rule three: don't piss frederick off. Go along with what he says, have dinner with him, tell him anything he wants to know, but don't give anything away. Lie. Embellish. Play up your broken heart.

SHE GLARED AT HIM, and he smiled, opening the back door of the limousine he was leaning against. "you look hungry, my beautiful padme. Allow me to buy you dinner."

She made an act of looking nervous and glancing around. Frederick pulled his coat aside and showed her his gun, then looked inside the bookstore, making his point. Padme sighed and climbed into the backseat of the car. Frederick got in beside her, too close. Padme heard the locks on the doors click shut. Despite herself, she shivered, and wondered if she would be able to fight him off if he tried anything.

Seeing her checking out potential escape routes, frederick reached into his pocket and pulled out a flick-knife. "try anything, padme, and i'll decorate the inside of this car with your blood."

Annoyed, rather than scared, padme's eyes narrowed. "do you get off on threatening people? Women?"

Frederick shrugged. "yes."

God. Padme looked away from his penetrating gaze. "what do you want?"

"storytime. I want to know how you and enver met. I know you were with him before you were his fbi. Protection. You were fucking each other in the four seasons hotel for two days straight. Did you know he was your protectee?"

Padme hated that she had to share this with this monster. It would sully her memory of that first weekend. She remembered dale's warning. Lie. Embellish. "yes, i knew. I went there to talk about the plan for monday."

"and you were seduced by him?"

She turned her usual warm brown eyes on him. Today, they were ice cold. "how do you know i didn't seduce him?"

Frederick smirked. "i don't. Bravo."

"i fucked him. But you already know that."

"so, let me get this straight. You're fresh out of quantico and you fuck your first assignment? Tell me, ms. Kaur, this self-destructive streak you have ..." he lunged for her suddenly, yanking her t-shirt up and bringing out the knife. He pressed the tip to her belly. "stop lying to me, padme, or i swear i will gut you right now. Did you know him before you fucked him?"

She shook her head, and he let her go. "that's better. Now, where did you meet?"

"a friend's party."

"and you went back to his hotel with him?"

She nodded. Frederick pulled her to him, and she cringed as he trailed his lips across her throat then up to her mouth. "mm, i can imagine it," he murmured, "his cock plunging into your silky cunt, reaming you into submission ... did you beg him not to stop, padme? Did you let him fuck you in whatever way he wanted?"

Padme felt sick and tried to wriggle away from him, but frederick merely laughed and locked his arms around her. "we're going to have a lovely meal, my beautiful padme, and then you will accompany me back to my hotel suite, and you will show me exactly how he made love to you."

Oh god, no ... she wrenched herself out of his arms, terrified and furious. "kill me. Kill me right now, frederick, because i will never, ever have sex with you."

Frederick threw his head back and laughed, reaching into his pocket. He pulled out his phone. "do you recognize this residence, padme?"

Every cell in her body went cold. Severin's house. She looked back at frederick's triumphant face. "don't. Don't hurt her." Her voice broke, which only made his smile bigger.

"guess we'll be spending the night together, then."

Padme closed her eyes. She felt frederick's mouth on hers. "kiss me back, padme. Make it convincing."

She obeyed, feeling a numbness creep over her. She instead switched off her feelings, become cold, stiff. Throughout dinner, she hardly ate anything, and when he held out his hand and led her to the elevator, she began to tremble. As the doors opened, she made to get in, but he stopped her.

"no."

Padme looked at him, confused. Frederick smiled, and the triumph in his eyes was more than she could bear. "i don't want toscano's sloppy seconds," he said. "you've proved to me that you're obedient, padme. You can go now."

Humiliation flooded through her body. Turn around, walk away. "you bastard," she hissed. "was anyone ever outside my mother's house?"

"oh, yes," he said. "i'll give you this. You're loyal. I would love to fuck you, padme, but as i said, you've been tainted by toscano. You can find your own way home."

He dismissed her with a wave and padme wished that she still had her fbi issue firearm on her. She would blow this cocksucker's brains out even if it meant a life sentence. She turned and started to walk away when he called her name.

"padme? I expect you to be at my beck and call if you want your loved ones to stay unharmed. Don't go disappearing on me. When i come to kill you, you had better be waiting and willing."

"fuck you," she said with tears in her eyes. "you won't get away with this."

She didn't hear his reply, the blood rushing in her ears was too loud. She went back onto the street and hailed a cab. To her relief, one pulled up almost immediately, a young woman at the wheel. Padme gave her the address gratefully and sat back. The driver was about her age, short dark hair cut into an efficient short bob, her body slender and athletic.

It was only when she realized the cab driver was taking an odd route to her apartment that she got nervous. She met the driver's eyes in the mirror and glared at her. "are you one of ingles' stooges too? Are you taking me somewhere to kill me and dump my body?"

The driver smirked. "quite the opposite, i can assure you, miss lemon."

Padme gave a small gasp. "enver?"

The driver nodded. "you're being followed; that's why i'm taking you elsewhere. I have a phone hook-up. You can speak to mr. Toscano."

Padme's heart soared, and she felt tears in her eyes. How quickly things changed. "is it safe?"

"it can only be a very brief, timed conversation. Then i will tell you anything you want to know. I have been told to share with you that your family and friends are also being watched by ingles' men—but in turn, they are being watched by a team of mr. Toscano's operatives. Your friends and your mother will not come to any harm."

Padme felt a weight lift from her shoulders. "so, i could leave the country, go to enver?"

The driver nodded. "but we must be careful, miss lemon." Padme smiled at the nickname. "we'll work out a plan for you to fly indirectly by setting up decoys and false trails. Mr. Toscano wants you to work with the fbi so that you have protection. He is concerned about your safety first and foremost. Frederick ingles has made you his only focus, and he's constantly watching."

Padme leaned forward. "you put a camera in my apartment."

"yes."

"can i ask your name?"

The driver hesitated and then nodded. "lisa."

Padme touched her shoulder. "thank you, lisa, for everything. Without you calling dale ..."

"just doing my job."

"what is your job, exactly?"

Lisa's eyes were guarded. "i'm mr. Toscano's associate. I fix things."

Padme nodded. "i get it."

"in the case under your seat, you'll find a .22. Keep it with you at all times."

Padme dug around for a small case and pulled out the .22. "you'll find it's been legally registered in your name," lisa continued. "there's spare ammo in the bag. Also, a burner phone with my number coded in. Only use it to call me, miss lemon."

"call me padme."

"padme. It's important that we do everything according to the plan. If successful, we could have you out of the country by the end of the week without ingles knowing. After your call tonight, i will drive you back to your apartment, where you will pack a bag. Then you will go to stay with your mother. From there we will body swap you with another young indian woman working for us, and you will be taken out of the country."

"to enver?"

"not directly. The ingles' influence is everywhere. So, you will fly to the first location with your own passport. That will lead ingles' men there, with any luck. While they are trying to find you, we will send out more decoys so that they catch your scent, as it were. In the meantime, you will be traveling to the next location under a different name and passport and so on and so on until we feel it's safe to reunite you with mr. Toscano. Understood?"

Padme couldn't help feeling excited. "and you're sure the people i love will be protected?"

Lisa smiled grimly. "oh, i am sure."

She drove them to a house outside the city. Inside, lisa set up the phone call. "we're having to reroute it a lot," she explained to padme. "if ingles' people even caught a whiff, they'd find him."

The second she heard enver's voice on the telephone, padme felt like bursting into tears. "pad?"

"oh, god, enver. Enver ..." her legs gave way and lisa steered her into a chair. "enver, i love you so much, god, i love you."

His voice was full of emotion. "as i love you, my darling one. I have missed you more than i can say. Are you okay? Are you all right? That terrible day ... i thought i'd lost you, but they wouldn't let me see you."

"i'm fine, totally fine. I just ...god, enver, it's been hell without you, not knowing if you were dead. I finally got what you were trying to tell me."

"i'm sorry we had to go through all that subterfuge—i apologize for having to drug you to get you to the hospital so we could get the last set of coordinates to you, but i was getting desperate. I knew ingles was honing in on you. He's reading your mail; he's bugging your calls. I'm so scared he'll try to kill ..." his voice choked off, and he couldn't finish what he was saying.

"fifty seconds," lisa said firmly. Padme started to panic. "we don't have long. Just know that i love you and i'm coming to be with you and we'll figure this out together."

"yes, we will. When we do, i'm going to marry you, padme kaur. What you have done for me, god, i love you."

Lisa was making a wind-up motion with her hand. "i have to go now, but i'll see you very soon. I love you, baby, so much."

"ti amo, padme kaur, ti amo. Trust lisa. She will do everything you need."

"soon, darling."

"soon."

The connection was broken, and padme felt bereft but happy. She handed lisa the phone. Lisa immediately took out the sim card and snapped it in two, then used her high heel to smash the phone. She bent over the laptop and typed in some code padme couldn't understand. Padme studied her. Everything about the other woman said efficiency and cool ruthlessness.

"are you military?"

Lisa smiled at her. "ex. I'm a freelancer now. Well, i say that, but i've been working for enver for about five years exclusively."

"he's a great guy." Padme felt a shared kinship with this woman because of her link to enver.

Lisa nodded. "he is. Forgive me, padme, but i don't even think you know just how great a guy he is."

Padme wasn't stung by the comment. "i know. Believe it or not, the thing i'm most looking forward to is getting to know him without any of this crap hanging over us."

Lisa nodded, her eyes sympathetic. "that's the hope, once we get you to the location. Padme, i've reached out to arlo forrester on enver's behalf, and so he knows what the situation is. He has unlimited resources, so he was the best option to help protect everybody. We agreed that between enver's men and arlo's security team, we can protect your mother, harpa and cosima, and your partner, dale, if necessary. I will be your protection until we can get you out of the country."

"you don't mind the babysitting job?"

Lisa grinned. "did you?"

Padme laughed. "no, but seeing you here today … i just realized that all those years training to be an agent were … not wasted, exactly, but i failed to see that it wasn't me. Which is scary, because i don't know what else is."

"you'll find your path. And listen, you took three bullets for enver. Was that all because you love him, or because your training kicked in?"

Padme considered and had to concede. "both."

"see? So, don't be down on yourself. You're what, twenty-eight? All due respect, but you're a baby. Plenty of time to find your calling."

Padme smiled at her, grateful for her kind words. "i kind of have a girl crush on you right now."

Lisa laughed. "well, i'm flattered. Look, let's get back to the apartment. I'll do a sweep of anything that might have been tampered with."

Padme blinked. "were you the one who drugged my orange juice?"

Lisa smiled sheepishly. "sorry. I needed to get you to a neutral place where ingles couldn't get in so we could deliver the last message. Until you knew where enver was, he didn't think you'd trust me to help you."

"i wouldn't have. I'm vaguely embarrassed you know about the lemon tattoo."

Lisa hitched up her top and showed padme a tattoo of dumbo. "courtesy of a bottle of tequila and a bad idea. So, we're even."

Padme laughed. God, she missed laughing. The last few months had been so stressful and painful, with everyone walking on egg shells around her.

"you mentioned dale. Does he know about you?"

Lisa shook her head. "and that's important—no one can know, pad. I know it will be painful, but i chose arlo because he has the resources and limitless money to fend off any attack. Dale fortuna is a good guy but no one, not even your mother, can know that you're leaving the country."

"okay." Padme let out a long breath and lisa studied her.

"if you're wondering if enver is worth it, i can tell you—he is. He adores you; he loves you totally. When you were shot, and we had to get him away, it took me and some huge guys to wrestle him onto a private jet. All he wanted was to be with you. We had to sedate him in the end."

"really?"

Lisa nodded. "his language when he woke up was beyond colorful." She laughed. "we finally got through to him when we got the news you were out of danger. It would have been dangerous for both of you if he'd come back to seattle."

Padme nodded. "i see that, and i'm glad he stayed away. It's easy to say now, but the last few months ... i've never known such pain, physically and emotionally."

Lisa put a hand on her arm. "you'll be together soon. Come on, let's go back to your apartment."

CHAPTER ELEVEN

It was two days later when lisa came to find padme at the bookstore. "can you get off work now? I need to talk to you."

Padme nodded. "i'll just see if beth can spare me."

In five minutes, they were walking down the block to a coffeehouse, not the same one she had gone to with ingles, but a more private, secluded one down an alleyway. They were the only customers, and so lisa kept her voice low and careful.

"pad, it's a go. We're going to be extracting you on friday." She flicked her eyes around the room. "this place is a cover. You'll come down here after your shift at the bookstore, grab a coffee, and then use the bathroom. We'll get you out from there. A decoy will be sent from here to trace your usual path back to your mom's place."

Padme, eyes wide, nodded. "good ...god, this is so quick."

Lisa studied her. "pad, we cannot risk any hint of suspicion on ingles' part. This means you can't say goodbye to anyone. Anyone. If your mom or any of your friends ask what your plans are for the weekend, you can make plans with them. Except, only you will know you won't be keeping them. Pad, we're going to be doing something that may upset you, but it's for your own safety, and for enver's. But it's a little, well, distasteful."

Padme searched lisa's eyes. "what?"

Lisa hesitated slightly. "pad, in a morgue in a private funeral home just outside seattle, there's a body of a murdered young indian american woman. This woman, she was stabbed, then pushed in front of a train. What's left of her, we'll use as your 'body'. We have a contact in the coroner's office, and we're going to need some of your dna."

"don't say it." Padme felt sick. "no. No, lisa. I can't do that to severin, to dale, to my friends. And what about the family of this poor girl?"

"she's a jane doe, pad."

Padme stared at lisa unhappily. "so, i would be 'dead'?"

Lisa nodded. "but, of course, that would mean ..."

"i could never come back, never see my mom, my friends again."

"but you and enver would be safe."

"you can't guarantee that."

"nothing is one hundred percent. Padme, i work for enver and by extension, as his partner, for you as well. I promise you this ... i will never, ever lie to you."

Padme gave a half smile. "so, if i asked you if you thought this was the right thing to do?"

"i would say yes. To keep you both safe and together for life."

Padme sat thinking for a while, then drew in a shaky breath. "okay. How does this work?"

Lisa gave her a smile. "you'll know on friday. I'm not risking any hint of this plan getting out. The moment you step into that bathroom, you will be under orders, okay? No arguing, no deviating from the plan. I'll be with you some of the way, but the last leg of your journey you'll be alone. We have all the travel documents you need."

. . .

On thursday night, padme went to dinner with her mother. Severin knew something was going on, but padme kept her word to lisa and said nothing. "just hormonal, mom," she told her with a half-smile when severin asked for the hundredth time if she was okay.

Severin had prepared a rack of succulent, delicious lamb, but padme found she had very little appetite. Severin studied her daughter with concern in her eyes. "pad, do you know how much you mean to me? If i had given birth to you, i could not love you more than i do."

Padme felt the tears coming. "mom ..."

"it breaks my heart to see you so ... broken. I can't bring enver back to you, but i wish i could. I see how much you love him."

Padme let the tears escape then, and let severin hold her. She let her think it was enver she was crying over rather than the fact she would never see severin again after tonight—that severin would have to go through the pain of thinking padme was dead.

Friday came, and padme went to work as normal. She was dressed in a sweater and jeans and her sneakers, her usual uniform to anyone's eye, but carefully chosen by lisa to match the decoys. Padme had gotten used to being 'escorted' to work by frederick ingles' men, and lisa had shown her how to spot them, keeping them in her peripheral vision while pretending to ignore their presence. Assholes.

Padme unclenched her jaw, rubbing her cheeks to ease the ache. She hadn't slept last night, and now she was hollow-eyed and exhausted. Being with enver still seemed so far away, and the thought of the possibility of many days traveling made her feel sick.

Beth frowned at her young friend when she saw her. "you don't look so good, pad. Are you sure you're up to working today?"

Padme nodded, half-smiling. "i am, beth, thanks. Just didn't sleep too well, is all."

Beth clearly wasn't convinced. "well, all right, but if you need a break, you go right ahead, okay?"

"will do."

It was almost lunchtime when padme felt the burner phone buzz in her pocket. She pulled it out to read the message.

Now.

She felt her adrenaline spike and looked around the store. It was empty, with only beth at the register, reading.

"beth? I might just run out for some coffee, if that's okay?"

Beth smiled at her. "sure, honey. Look, it's dead in here today, why don't you take off for the day?"

"are you sure?"

"very." Beth came to hug padme and padme clung to her.

"thank you, beth. For everything. I mean it."

Beth released her and frowned. "are you sure you're okay?"

Padme felt her eyes fill with tears. "i'm not, but i will be. Thanks, beth."

Padme left the bookstore and walked slowly down to the coffeehouse, feeling ingles' men following her. She wasn't worried. They never came in, just waited for her outside. She pulled her baseball cap down over her eyes and went into the café. She ordered her usual vanilla latte and turned to find a table at the back to wait for lisa's signal.

To her horror, frederick ingles was behind her. He smiled at her. "hello again, padme. Would you join me?"

Oh, fuck. Padme felt panic well up inside her, but she kept her face expressionless. "and what if i say i'd rather not?"

He stepped closer and lowered his voice. "then i'd say i'd hate to ruin that pretty gray t-shirt you're wearing."

Padme felt him press something to her—she didn't need to look down to see it was a knife. "fine."

They sat down, and he studied her. "you look tired. Beautiful, but tired."

"what do you want, ingles?"

"just your company for a few minutes, my dear. Checking in, you know? Wanting to know how you're spending your last days."

She met his gaze. "why not just kill me? I'm tired of all your empty threats, ingles. Either kill me or leave me alone."

Frederick chuckled. "i have to say the temptation to drive this knife into your exquisite body grows more acute every day, but i'm enjoying the anticipation. And there's the risk that toscano will disappear for good if he knows you're already dead. No, i want him to be watching when i kill you."

Padme was amazed that she didn't feel scared anymore, that she was growing immune to the horror of this man. "answer me something. The testimony enver gave, it put your operatives away, perhaps lost you some business, some government contracts. But i've done my research, ingles. You may have lost face, but you're still worth billions. Why not enjoy that and let it drop?"

Frederick's eyes were alive with anger. "honor." His voice was crackling with dangerous energy. "toscano thought he could take me down?"

"he did. And to be honest, he succeeded, didn't he? What are you now, ingles? Little more than a poor little rich boy acting out. Go home, ingles. Live your life. This insane revenge plan will only end one way."

He moved so quickly that no one could have stopped him. He lunged for her and grabbed her throat. Padme heard the barista shout "hey!" In alarm.

Frederick slammed padme against the wall, his fingers squeezing her throat. "you little whore," he spat. "what do you know about me? I am an ingles."

She felt the tip of the knife press against her belly. "do it," she said in a low steady voice. "kill me. Because i swear to you, ingles, this will be your last chance."

Ingles' face was red with fury, and for a second, padme thought he might go through with it. Then they both heard the click of a safety being flicked off.

"you will take your hands off of her, right now, ingles, or i swear to god, your brains will decorate the wall." Dale's voice was hard, unflinching.

Slowly, ingles released her and she slipped away from him. Frederick turned and faced dale, whose gun was still aimed at his head. "just a misunderstanding, agent."

Dale put his gun down, but didn't holster it. "pad, you okay?"

"i'm fine."

"you want to press charges?"

Padme hesitated. "no. I think mr. Ingles got the message." The last thing she needed right now was to go down to the field office to make a statement. She was already late for lisa. "have you got this? I need to go use the bathroom, straighten myself up."

Dale nodded, throwing her a smile. "i got this."

DALE EYED frederick ingles. "from now, ingles, you stay away from padme, got it? If i hear you're harassing her again, we got a problem, understand?"

"you're pretty full of yourself for a rookie agent," frederick said, his tone light but undercut with annoyance.

Dale didn't rise to the bait. "get out of here before i go against pad's wishes and haul your ass to jail."

Fredrick smirked but picked up his coffee and drained it. "i'll see you soon, officer."

And he was gone.

Dale holstered his weapon, checking around the coffee house, seeing wide-eyed, frightened customers. "relax, folks, he's gone."

The barista pushed a coffee towards dale. "on the house, fella, and thanks."

Dale grinned. "thank you. Mind if i hang out, wait for my friend?"

"no problem. Hope she's okay."

Dale grinned. "pad's suffered worse than that and survived. She'll be fine."

Ten minutes later, dale checked his watch. He got up and spoke to one of the female baristas. "hey, would you mind going into the ladies' bathroom and checking on my friend?"

"sure thing." The young woman pushed her way into the bathroom and in a flash, was out again. "there's no one in there."

Dale pushed past her and checked the place. Empty. At the far end, a fire door swung open and shut in the breeze.

"fuck!" Dale yanked his phone out of his pocket. "yeah, fortuna here. I need to report an abduction. Frederick ingles has padme kaur."

12

CHAPTER TWELVE

Lisa listened to what padme was telling her as they traveled to the airport. Lisa nodded. "believe it or not, that might help us. They might think ingles took you, which would mean he might be arrested. That gives us more time to get you out of the country and to enver."

The first leg of the journey was down to rio. "we're trying to avoid europe as much as possible," lisa explained, "as most of ingles' reach is there. South america and asia, and a rather annoying new zealand-japan-australia leg, are a possibility. Until we're sure you're not being followed, we keep moving."

Padme nodded, already feeling wiped out. "i'll do whatever it takes to keep enver safe."

"and you, too, pad," lisa reminded her gently, and padme squeezed her hand.

"i can never repay what you have done for me, lisa. You are a true friend."

"STILL THINK I'M A FRIEND?" Lisa asked with a grin fifty-six hours later after they'd flown from rio to jakarta to nairobi. They were waiting in nairobi for the next flight to hong kong.

Hollowed and high from sheer exhaustion, padme laughed and cried at the same time. "the insides of my eyelids are sparkling," she said, blinking a few times. Lisa looked sympathetic and annoyingly refreshed.

"i don't usually condone this sort of thing, but i have an ambien you can take. The next leg, we booked you in business class—with a bed. I'm not a monster, you need to sleep even if we're dragging you all over the globe."

Padme shook her head in wonder. "how do you look so good?"

"i have a backup. I sleep when they take over."

Padme bugged at her. "when the hell did that happen?"

Lisa chuckled. "they've been with us the whole time. At least thirty on each flight."

"and we've flown at least first class all the way. Jesus, how does enver afford it? I have most of his money at the moment."

Lisa shook her head. "no, pad. You hardly have any of it."

Padme was quiet after that. She knew enver was rich, of course, a billionaire, but to say that she had not even a fraction of his worth when there was nearly a billion sitting in her checking account ... that blew her mind.

"i need to find a way of transferring that back to him," she said to lisa, who shook her head.

"no, look, pad, enver wanted ...god, how do i say this? They'll think you're dead, and hopefully they'll charge ingles with your murder, and then this can all go away. But your mother, enver wanted her to have something. Something to help protect her, you know? I assume you had a will?"

Padme couldn't help feeling uncomfortable. "so, it's like he bought me from her?"

"i can see how that might be a concern, or what some people

might think, but no. Don't think of it as compensation, think of it as a necessity."

Padme was silent then, and soon they were being boarded on their next flight. Padme almost swooned at the soft bed she was given, and lisa chuckled as she handed over the ambien and a glass of water. "sleep, girl. I have a feeling this will all be over soon."

Padme fell asleep as soon as her head touched the pillow.

When she awoke, she looked out of the window and saw land. "hey, you, i thought i heard you get up." Lisa poked her head around the seat. "we're nearly landed."

"how long have i been out?"

"almost a day." Lisa grinned when she saw padme's surprise. "hey, you didn't miss anything. Except for maybe a really lame in-flight movie."

Padme rubbed her eyes. "where are we? What's next?"

Lisa smiled. "the last leg."

"really?" Padme was shocked and delighted, and lisa laughed. "really. We have the all clear. Enver's private plane is waiting for you at hong kong. It'll take you to where he is."

"you're not coming with me?"

Lisa shook her head. "no, i'll do a bit more traveling with your decoy to really make sure we're home and clear."

Padme wanted to cry she was so happy. "i can't believe we did it. Every step, i was waiting for ingles' men to catch up to us."

Lisa nodded somberly. "you weren't the only one. What i think we forget in this melee is that he is only one man. He's the last of the ingles—if he's toppled, their whole house of cards falls down and there are plenty of underworld families ready to see that day, believe me. His blind vengeance will mean his demise, pad, i promise you that. It's my job to make sure he doesn't take you and enver with him."

Padme regarded her friend with worried eyes. "you will take care of yourself, too, right?"

"you know i will."

Relieved, padme grinned. "because if i end up marrying enver, i'm going to need a maid of honor."

"just don't expect me to wear a dress."

"peach meringue. Eighties' style."

"i have a loaded weapon, kaur."

They both laughed, and padme grabbed lisa in a bear hug. The other woman squeezed her hard. "i'm happy for you, pad. You both deserve every happiness."

13

CHAPTER THIRTEEN

Padme's heart was beating almost out of her chest as the car approached the small house at the far end of the island. After all the shenanigans getting here, in a few short moments she would finally, finally see him.

Her legs shook as she got out of the car and then the door of the house flew open, and there was enver, all beauty and love. He was running to her, taking her in his arms. The moment his lips met hers, padme felt the pain of the last few months fall away. Her cheeks were wet with tears.

"enver, oh god, enver." His arms were tight around her as he gazed deep into her eyes. Time and distance had not made him any less glorious than she remembered. His bright green eyes were soft with love, his dark hair wild about his head, a dark beard on his gorgeous face.

"il mia amore, il mia amore ..." he kissed her again and again until she was breathless and laughing with joy. He swept her up in his arms and carried her inside the house. Padme saw that the silent driver had already brought her suitcases in and disappeared. She couldn't stop looking at enver's face, touching him, because she couldn't believe he was real.

Enver strode straight to the bedroom, padme still in his arms, and she giggled as he laid her on the bed and covered her body with his. "no staff?"

Enver grinned. "just us, cara mia. God, i've missed you."

She smoothed his curls away from his face. "i love you, enver toscano. Promise me we'll never be apart again."

"i promise you that, with all my heart." His hands were at the buttons of her dress, and she smiled as he bent his head to kiss her mouth, her throat, pulling down the lacy cup of her bra to take her nipple into his mouth. "and you should also know, my darling padme, that i'm not letting you up from this bed for at least the next twenty-four hours."

The months of longing made both of them tear at each other's clothes, but the smile on enver's face faded when he saw the scars from her bullet wounds.

"mio dio ..." he stroked each one gently and closed his eyes. Padme could see the pain on his face.

"hey," she stroked his cheek, "it's okay. I'm okay. I'm here."

She pulled his head down and pressed her lips against his, their tongues caressing. Enver's fingers strummed a blissful rhythm on her clit, while she freed his diamond-hard cock from his jeans.

"don't wait," she said, breathlessly. "i need you so badly."

Smiling, he hitched her legs around his waist and thrust into her with one hard push. Padme's head rolled back as she gasped with pleasure, enver's lips against her throat.

"look at me," he said, and she met his gaze as he pinned her hands to the bed, and padme tightened her vaginal muscles around his huge cock. "that's it, beautiful, let me fuck you."

They found their rhythm as if they had never been apart, a meeting of equals, both absorbing the other's cries and gasps for breath. "i love you," padme told enver over and over then as she came, her back arched up, her belly pressed against his.

"mio dio, sei così cazzo bella," enver panted as he neared his own peak. "you're so fucking beautiful."

He came with a long groan, his seed pumping deep into her belly as she clamped her thighs around him, keeping him locked inside her. Enver made no move to withdraw as they collapsed to the bed, instead holding her close to him, showering her with kisses until she started giggling uncontrollably.

His cock grew hard again inside of her, and they made love slowly, talking softly to each other, exploring the other's bodies.

It was evening before they paused, showering together before enver showed her around the small property. It was everything a beach villa should be, glass walls, wooden floors painted white. It was simple, elegant, and cozy.

Padme sat in the large kitchen while enver cooked steaks for their supper. "can i help at all?"

Enver grinned. "no way. You've had a long journey, and i want you to save your energy for what i'm going to do to you tonight."

Padme grinned. "i still can't believe i'm here, that i'm with you again. Jesus, enver, these last few months have been hell."

His smile faded, and he cupped her cheek in his hand. "i know, and i'm sorry. Did lisa tell you that i wasn't a willing abductee?"

Padme giggled. "she did. She's badass."

"she is."

Padme choked back a laugh. "you're scared of her."

Enver grinned wryly. "terrified. But she's been my rock. She spends evenings listening to me talk endlessly about you. Did you like her?"

"very much. She calls me lemon."

Enver laughed. "who said hired mercenaries don't have a sense of humor?"

"a mercenary? Even more badass. She makes me realize i was never cut out to be an fbi agent."

Enver shook his head. "i disagree, but selfishly, i'm glad you're no longer an agent. The thought of you putting yourself in danger again ..." he shook his head, remembering. "i'll never forget that day you were shot, cara mia, never. And they dragged me away from you, and i thought you were dead. Christ. There was so much blood, your precious blood, everywhere."

Padme felt a wave of nausea go through her at the memory, but she shook her head. "come back to this moment, enver. We're here. We're safe, and together."

"yes." He leaned over to kiss her. "and we need to start to figure out where our lives are going now. Sound like fun?"

Padme grinned. "hell, yes." She tangled her fingers in his dark hair, gazing up at him. "we have the time to get to know each other properly now."

He was silent for a moment, then kissed her softly before speaking. "padme, you have given up everything for me. I hope i prove to be worth your sacrifice."

"i have no doubts," she said firmly. "none. All i want is to be with you."

Enver smiled, but his eyes were still wary. "principessa, soon you may want more. A new career, new friends. All i am saying is, please be honest if ever you should find yourself unhappy."

"i will, i promise, and in turn i hope i prove that i'm enough for you, enver. You had this life, this amazing, successful life and you gave it up to try and do the right thing. I can't tell you how much i admire you."

Enver pulled her into his arms, tumbling her to the floor of the kitchen, and she could feel his cock hard against her thigh. "you could show me," he said with a grin as she wrapped her arms around his waist. He reached down to unzip his pants and seconds later thrust into her again. Padme gasped and laughed as he began to move inside her.

"god, that feels so good, so good ... enver, enver ... enver ..."

Severin's legs gave way, and she sank to the floor. "no ... no ..."

Dale could barely keep his own emotions under control. "i'm so sorry, sev, so sorry."

Henry was holding the older woman's hands. "there's no need for you to identify padme. The coroner has already matched her dna to the body."

Severin's tears were pouring down her face. "how? How did she die?"

Henry looked at dale. "dale?"

"she was ...god, i'm sorry, sev ... she was stabbed repeatedly, then thrown in front of a train. The wounds on her body ... it matches frederick ingles' m.o. we're bringing him in for questioning."

"that son-of-a-bitch!" Severin was up then, looking between the men. "let me at him. Please, for five minutes, with a baseball bat."

"i truly wish we could allow that," henry said, his kind eyes sad. "severin, when the medical examiner has finished his investigation, we think it best if you have a closed casket funeral for padme."

Severin stared at henry as if she couldn't believe a word he was saying. "i'll decide my daughter's funeral arrangements, thank you, henry."

"of course. I apologize. I meant well."

Severin squeezed her eyes shut. "i can't believe she's dead."

"we'll make ingles pay for this," henry patted her hand. "i swear we will."

Henry spoke quietly to dale on his way out. "stay with her, won't you? I think she'll need her friends around her."

Dale nodded. "i wanna kill ingles, henry. I wanna rip him to pieces with my bare hands."

"you and me both, dale."

Severin was standing at the window when dale returned with a hot cup of tea. She accepted it, murmuring her thanks. Dale waited for her to speak.

"i don't believe it, dale," severin said eventually. "i keep going through it in my mind over and over. No one saw her being taken from the coffeehouse. She would have fought, screamed, yelled."

"that's what bugs me too, sev. Unless she was drugged or ... god, i don't know. But i think i agree with you. This stinks, but i can't put my finger on why."

"she's not dead," severin shook her head then turned to dale. "i want to see the body."

Dale went cold. "no, god, sev ... the body is ... it's not padme anymore. The head is gone, the torso so badly damaged that they didn't notice the stab wounds at first. Her limbs were pulverized. It isn't padme."

"that's what i'm saying. I'll know. Fuck dna; they've messed that up. It's not padme. I want to see the body."

Dale stared at her unhappily but then nodded. "okay. But it'll have to be off the books. I'll get you in, but we'll have to do it under cover of night."

Severin nodded, her expression set and determined. "let's keep this just between us, dale. Don't even tell henry."

Dale's face was grim. "i agree. Just you and me."

PADME OPENED HER EYES. The sun was warm against the bare skin of her back, and enver was trailing a cool fingertip up and down her spine. She smiled up at him. His dark curls had grown wild around his head in the month since she'd been here, and he looked boyish and relaxed. She realized that, in their time before the shooting, he had always appeared relaxed but he'd had a tension about him, even in their most intimate moments. Here in their small hideaway, he was completely himself.

Their love had only grown more complete, more intense as they spent all day, every day together. They learned about each other's hopes and dreams—which, of course, were mostly based on being with each other and making a family.

"i want ... twelve." Enver nodded sagely, only his crinkled eyes giving away that he was joking.

Padme giggled. "then you can push them out of your wang, because my va-jay-jay ain't happy with that."

"six sets of twins?"

He tickled her as they laughed. There was a rainstorm outside, and they lounged around on the huge white sofas, a lazy afternoon. Padme kissed the tip of his nose. "i love you, but no."

"okay, i'll settle for two."

"that's more like it. Girls or boys."

"one of each."

"that's fair, but boring."

"sorry, cara mia." He grinned as she slid her hands under his shirt. "now, how about animals?"

Padme's eyes lit up. "dogs. Lots of dogs."

"so, you want a lot of dogs, but only two kids?"

"i don't have to give birth to dogs," she nodded in mock-seriousness and he laughed.

"fair enough." He studied her—padme seemed lost in thought. "what is it?"

"just picturing two little tykes with your curls running around yelling in italian, chasing our many dogs."

"and where do you see this scene?"

"italy," she said firmly. "enver, in my dreams, we make a life in the italian countryside, or on the coast, or even in a small town. I can see it so vividly it seems real. I just know we'll get there someday. I love it here, don't think i don't, but our true life, our own story, won't begin until this is all over. We can sit here in paradise and pretend, but ..."

"i know, baby. But it's too dangerous at the moment. Ingles has told you to your face he intends to kill you."

"and you."

"i'm more concerned about you. For me, it'll be a bullet to the head. Over quick. When it comes to women, ingles is a sadist. You think those bullets were painful? Look what he did to chaley."

"i know what he'll do to me," padme said. "i'm just frustrated. Why should we let him dictate our lives? We need to confront him."

"we tried that, remember? Until we have a strong lead on how to bring him down, i won't risk your life."

Padme sighed. "fine."

"don't be sad, pad. How can i make you happy?" But his hand was already snaking under her t-shirt, his warm fingers caressing her belly. She smiled up at him.

"keep going ... i see your other hand is free—get it busy, man."

Enver laughed, his green eyes twinkling at her as his other hand deftly unbuttoned her denim shorts. Soon both hands were tugging them down, along with her panties, and his mouth had found her clit. Padme gave a moan of pleasure as his tongue twisted and lashed around her, her hands tangling in his dark curls.

"enver, let me taste you too."

Not stopping his assault on her sex, he turned, and she freed his cock from his linen trousers and took it into her mouth. God, he was so big and hard already, and she traced the tip of her tongue along the long shaft, feeling it quiver under her touch. He tasted of salt and soap, the silky skin of his cock belying the rock-hard muscle beneath. They teased and sucked and licked at each other until they were both moaning and coming.

Enver's hissed, triumphant moan of "yes, cara mia, yes!" Was all padme needed to hear to bring her to climax. She came, arching her back but still working on him until he came in her mouth, hot, creamy cum spilling onto her tongue.

Breathless, enver moved so he could kiss her mouth. "god, padme, you're so fucking sexy, it kills me. Baby, will you touch yourself for me so i can watch you?"

She nodded. "if you do the same."

"can i come on your belly?"

She nodded eagerly, and enver sat on his haunches as she slid her hand between her legs and began to rub her clit, never taking her eyes from his. Enver fisted the root of his cock, already stiffening again as he watched her.

"i love the way your body moves, those beautiful breasts, your soft belly ... those thighs ... god ... your exquisite face ..."

He began to pant as he pulled and stroked himself, his eyes taking her in, the flush of her skin, her hand moving on her sex, how red and swollen her labia were, her arousal obvious. "mio dio, padme ... i'm going to fuck you in every way tonight ... every way ..."

Padme came quickly, crying out his name again and again, her body undulating with her movements and when enver came a moment later, his seed spilling onto her belly, she was so aroused that the moment his hand touched her clit she came again, making them both laugh. They got their breath back and his cock was inside her, the two of them moving together in rhythm, each focusing entirely on the other.

"enver?"

"yes, il mia amore?"

Padme pulled his head down to kiss him. "i love you. There isn't a way to tell you how much; there are no words. You are my life."

"and you are mine, cara mia ... the only thing in this world i care about. The only one i will ever want ..."

As the rain lashed down outside, they forgot about the outside world—forgot about eating or sleeping and the rest of their worries. They made love long into the night until, exhausted and sated, they fell asleep in each other's arms.

DALE OPENED the door but then shut it quickly, having second thoughts. He turned to severin. "i'll ask one last time. Are you sure?"

Severin was pale, her usually radiant dark skin almost gray. "i'm sure."

Dale led her into the morgue and checked the number on the door. He pulled out number three, balking again at the cover on the body—or what was left of it. He looked up at severin, who nodded and took a deep breath in. Dale lifted the cover and heard severin's gasp of distress. The headless torso was badly mangled, but the medical examiner had cleaned it and the stab wounds in the abdomen were obvious, crisscrossing across the center of the belly, slicing through the navel. Dale had seen the same pattern of wounds on chaley saunders' body. Vicious, brutal and merciless, inflicted to cause maximum pain. The body's limbs were crushed but intact, and slowly severin picked up the right hand and cradled it in hers. For a few minutes, she studied it, then closed her eyes, her lips moving in a silent prayer.

"the doctor did say he thought she was already dead when

she was thrown in front of the train. They interviewed the driver, who said he just saw a flash of something being pushed out. He had no time to stop. He's pretty destroyed, poor guy. Doc said her abdominal artery was severed in the stabbing; she would have bled out in minutes." Dale swallowed the bile in his throat. "sev?"

"this isn't my daughter," she said quietly. "it isn't padme."

"sev ..."

She opened her eyes and smiled sadly at him. "when she was shot by brian dedalus, i spent weeks at her hospital bedside holding her right hand. Weeks, dale. I got to know that hand very well. She has a mole on the joint between her finger and thumb. Next to it, so small you would never know if you hadn't seen her hand up close, is a small strawberry birthmark. This poor young woman doesn't have the mole or the birthmark. It isn't padme, and now i'm wondering why henry jones is so convinced it is."

Dale stared at her. "you're sure?"

"never more so."

Dale chewed over this information in his mind. It had been henry who had told him the dna was padme's; henry who had spoken to the medical examiner without him. Henry who had questioned, then released, ingles without charge. All of which was fine, and above board ... except this wasn't padme. Dale believed severin with all his heart. Another thing suddenly occurred to him.

"the bullet wounds." He gestured to the torso. "where padme was shot, there's flesh taken from those sites externally, but then there's no mention of internal scar tissue from the bullet path. Jesus." He felt his body begin to quiver. "jesus. None of this makes sense, sev. Why would henry be so eager to pronounce this body as pad's? And why the hell would the medical examiner go along with it? This stinks."

Severin was studying him. "maybe he helped her leave the country. Hell, that's what i would have done. He's been her mentor, her friend since she was a teenager. If anyone could get her safely out of the country, it's him. Do we say we know?"

Dale shook his head. "if he arranged this body to look like pad's, it may be to throw ingles off her scent, so i think our best plan is to keep the status quo. We need to be the devastated mother and friend. We need to have that funeral, even if the casket is empty. Jesus, yes, that's why henry said a closed casket —it all makes sense now. Shit, why didn't i think of it?"

Severin smiled, the light back in her eyes. "she's alive, dale. She's alive and safe and happy with enver. I know it with every bone in my body."

Dale nodded, a hopeful smile on his handsome face. "you're right, sev. Padme's alive."

14

CHAPTER FOURTEEN

Dale didn't feel as happy on the day of the funeral. Severin played her part almost too well, utterly distraught, but it was padme's friends, the ones who didn't know she was alive, that he felt for. Harpa malhotra was inconsolable, sobbing openly, her beautiful elder sister cosima trying to comfort her through her own sadness. Mikah ray looked shattered; arlo forrester's face was stone-like and gray with distress. Beth, padme's employer at the bookstore, held severin's hand, looking older than her years, grief making her seem bent and elderly. Dale read a small poem, his voice breaking before henry took the podium.

"ten years," he began, coughing to hide the break in his voice. "ten years ago, i met a young eighteen-year-old woman. She almost ran into my car on her bicycle and she, well, she cussed me out. The sight of this beautiful young indian american girl angry with me ... that day it just made me laugh, especially the salty language coming out of her mouth. I started to laugh. I can't even tell you why. She just stared at me for a long moment, then burst out laughing too. We were fast friends ever since that moment. I saw in padme something i rarely see: joie de vivre, a joy of life. Given her upbringing, the abandonment by her birth parents, she could so easily have gone to the dark side, but she never did. When she found her true mother, severin, something was set off inside her—a spark. A spark, a will to better herself, to become what her intelligence, her street smarts, and her warmth promised. She exceeded all of that promise. She found great happiness with a remarkable man, and it is a tragedy that they were torn apart and that they were not reunited before this terrible ending."

Dale closed his eyes, trying not to focus on the pain in his chest. It's not real, it's not real. She's alive, somewhere. He wanted desperately to believe it entirely, but until he could confirm that she was still alive and not being held against her will, he had to hold back his excitement. If ingles still had her, dale was sure that he was inflicting great torture on her—and he would have no intention of letting her go alive.

Which meant only one thing. Dale had to go and find out for himself. He had to find ingles.

HARPA MALHOTRA DIDN'T HAVE any tears left. She moved around the empty kitchen of her restaurant, closed 'due to bereavement.' and wondered if she would ever feel normal again. Padme was dead. Harpa and padme had been as close as sisters and now ... cosima knocked at the open door.

"hey, sis."

She wrapped her arms around harpa. Harpa leaned into her older sister, breathing in her clean, comforting scent. "i can't believe she's gone, cos."

"i know, harp. It's unreal."

Harpa wiped her eyes. "god, i feel like i did when you got shot. Hopeless. Directionless."

Cosima nodded, her lovely face creased with concern. "i

wish i could say it gets better." She glanced at her watch. "sweetie, i'm so sorry, but i have to get back for the kids. Want to come with me?"

Harpa smiled but shook her head. "mikah's coming to get me in a half-hour. Kiss the kids for me."

"i will. Love you."

"love you too, sis."

It was eerily quiet after cosima left and harpa wondered if she shouldn't just call mikah to come get her early. She decided to take the trash out of the back door and wedged it open with a block of wood. She dumped the bag in the dumpster and turned to go back inside.

Two huge men were behind her and she started in alarm. One of them grabbed her, the other twisted a rope around her neck.

"no," she croaked as the rope tightened and he began to choke her. "please, god, no ..."

"shut the fuck up, bitch. This ain't personal. It's to send a message to your whore friend."

Harpa was unable to struggle against the sheer bulk of her captors and she began to pass out. As she fainted, she heard a shout, a familiar voice. "mikah," she gasped, then everything went dark.

When she awoke, she was being cradled in mikah's arms in the back of arlo's suv. She blinked and drew in a deep breath. "mikah?"

His face was drawn, pale and angry. "it's okay, sweetheart, we're taking you to the emergency room."

"no," she struggled and sat up, touching her bruised throat. "i'm okay. What happened to those animals?"

"we're going to the er, even it's just to check you out," arlo said from the front seat. Cosima was next to him, and she turned to take her sister's hand. Harpa saw her face was tear-stained.

"mikah and arlo and some guys from the street managed to grab them. We called the police, and the guys said they'd take care of it. Oh, sweetie, if only i hadn't left you."

Harpa felt mikah stroke her hair. "it's okay, really. I'm okay, just a bit sore. They said they were doing it to send a message to my 'whore friend.' what the hell? I'm assuming they meant pad and that they worked for ingles, but he already killed her. Why is he sending goons after me to send a message?"

Mikah and cosima shook their heads, but harpa caught arlo's eye in the rearview mirror. He gave an almost imperceptible shake of his head. Harpa struggled to hide her gasp. Arlo knew something. Was padme alive?

Harpa changed the subject. "i really don't need the er. I actually don't think they meant to kill me, just hurt me enough to send a warning."

"er," mikah said firmly, and she acquiesced. The more she complied, the more chance she would get to ask arlo what the hell was going on.

DESPITE HER HAPPINESS, enver knew padme still felt pain. Pain at missing severin and her friends, pain at leaving dale behind. Enver would catch her staring out at the sea, pensive and sad. He wished he could do something to ease her pain for her. She had asked him about the lack of phones and laptops in their home and enver had been honest.

"first, because any internet supply can be hacked and we could be traced. Second, it's to stop you brooding. I know you want to know how your family is, and it's understandable, but it will drive you crazy. I know this for a fact because i was going crazy all the time we were separated. It was lisa who eventually took my stuff away. She left me with the camera feed for a couple of hours each week and i would watch you. I know that sounds so creepy, but that's why i only had the one camera in your living room. No, it still sounds creepy," he said with a laugh and she had to join in.

"it's okay—i was just glad it was you and not ingles. Once i knew it was there, it was a comfort. Did you see me telling you i loved you?"

Enver nodded, smiling. "a couple of times."

Padme thought back and laughed. "i had this plan—because we didn't know if ingles had bugged the place after dale had checked—that i would 'read' certain books with titles that spelled out a message. I bought bagfuls, but i never got around to doing it."

"inventive." Enver was grinning at her, and she threw a pillow at him.

"what about you? That whole money and lotto ticket thing? I have to say, it took me a while."

"not really. After you got the lotto ticket, you pretty much figured it out."

"why the delay between the two? I mean, you transferred the money almost the day after the shooting and then waited for six months,"

Enver rubbed his hands on his head. "the money was genuinely to help you. In fact, i almost just put a random amount into your bank account until the idea came to me. The only person i told was lisa and she advised me to wait to give you the other coordinate because you were being watched. Also, pad, you needed to heal." He was looking sick again, thinking about her shooting.

Padme pulled him down onto the couch with her and wrapped her arms and legs around him. "you're trapped until you smile." She nibbled at his ear with her teeth and nipped his bottom lip.

Enver smiled but she didn't release him and he slid his

hand down to her groin. "sexy times." She grinned at him, then gave a sigh of pleasure as his fingers made contact with her clit through her pants. "i'll never get tired of touching you, beautiful girl," he said, and kissed her, his tongue caressing hers. She smiled up at him, her eyes alive with desire and mischief.

"good. Now put that huge cock in me, soldier ..."

DALE BACKED into the door of his apartment, carrying the pizza box and six-pack of beer. He needed an evening of something other than obsessing over padme, a night to himself. Damn, he hadn't even been on a real date in years. He knew some of his friends thought it was because he was in love with padme, but that couldn't be further from the truth. He loved her as his partner and his best friend, but he had never thought of her in that way.

He turned on his tv to watch the game, and ate his body weight in carbs. Just after eleven p.m., he was napping when he heard the door being kicked in. He reached for his weapon but was too late. The man with the tire iron made contact with dale's head just as his fingers touched the grip.

PADME FELT a lurch in her stomach and slid from the bed. It was just before dawn and enver was asleep beside her. The house was silent as she padded barefoot to the bathroom.

She felt another lurch as she reached it, and dashed for the toilet. She threw up, feeling sweat break out on her skin. God, please don't let me be sick. She dry heaved a couple of times, but it soon passed. She brushed her teeth and splashed water on her face, then sat on the edge of the bath. Maybe she was due for her period—she always felt a little feverish the few days before. She tried to work out when she'd last had her cycle and then she gasped. No. No way.

It was three weeks late. She had been here on the island for a month and she and enver hardly ever used condoms because she was on the pill.

Except, dumbass, you'd only just started taking it again the day you found out enver was alive and that you'd be reunited. Oh fuck. She knew in her bones that it was true.

She was pregnant.

15

CHAPTER FIFTEEN

Cold water was thrown on him and dale woke with a start, his head screaming with pain. He could taste blood. He opened his eyes. He was in the backroom of some sleazy club, or so he thought from what he could make out. Frederick ingles sat in a chair, watching him.

"good evening, agent fortuna. I only have one question for you, and how you decide to answer it will determine how merciful i'll be when it comes time to kill you."

"fuck you, ingles."

Frederick's smile was chilly. "where is padme kaur, agent fortuna?"

Dale spat out a mouthful of blood. "in the ground, where you put her, asshole."

"i don't think so. I'll ask again. Where is padme?"

"my answer is the same."

Frederick cleared his throat, and one of his goons landed a kick to the side of dale's head. Dale groaned in agony but righted himself. "you murdered her, ingles, and you know it. You stuck a knife in her gut then threw her body in front of the seven a.m. To portland."

"hmm." Frederick leaned forward in his chair. "the only problem is that i know for sure the women you peeled up from the tracks wasn't padme kaur. She looked like her, certainly; she was beautiful and sweet. But it wasn't padme. I know because i killed your stand-in. The dead girl was my practice run for how i'm going to kill padme when i find her. Slowly. Painfully. And you're going to help me make that happen."

"fuck you. I'm not telling you anything. You'll just have to kill me."

Frederick stared at him for what seemed an age and then shrugged. "okay."

And dale waited for the killer blow.

THE GARBAGE DIVER moved slowly through the piles of trash, trying to pick out anything he could use or sell or eat. When he saw the young man sprawled unconscious, face-down in the stinking pile, he was certain, for sure, that he must be dead. The guy was covered in blood, for one. The garbage man looked around and poked the dead guy. The dead guy moaned, and the garbage man jumped back, then sighed.

Yesterday, a sympathetic woman had given him some change, and he'd had a hot dog and burger from a street vendor. Now he had just a few cents left. He was going to have to use them to call an ambulance, wasn't he?

PADME DIDN'T KNOW how to tell enver she was having his baby. It was such a bad time to bring a child into the world—as much as they kidded themselves, they knew they both had targets on their back and padme could not even think of her and enver's child being exposed to that kind of danger. She could only be month along, at most. Maybe the best thing would be to get it taken care of before it grew into a human, but they were on an island in the middle of nowhere. She didn't even know if abortion was legal in the maldives, and didn't know how she could find out without access to the internet.

"lisa is coming to see us," enver said as they sat at breakfast. Padme was surprised.

"how do you know?"

"we have our methods of communication," he said cagily, and padme rolled her eyes and muttered something about 'james bond.' enver grinned.

"you know it. Anyway, she's doing the decoy travel thing, but she'll be here by the end of the week."

Padme smiled. "it will be good to see her, i have to admit. I assume i'm not allowed to ask her about back home?"

Enver hesitated, but then relented. "you can ask, but it doesn't mean she'll tell you."

When lisa arrived, she was grim-faced, but hugged padme. "your mom is fine, pad. She's obviously distressed and grieving, but she's safe. Arlo has organized some hardcore protection for everyone."

Enver saw padme's shoulders slump with relief. "thank god. Thank you, lisa."

"you're welcome, lemon." The two women smiled at each other. "hey, you mind if i steal enver for a few? Business stuff."

"of course. Look, you must be hungry, i'll make us some supper." Padme threw enver a smile, then disappeared.

Enver could see lisa had bad news for him. He nodded outside. "come see the beach."

They walked a little way from the house so they couldn't be overheard. Lisa looked at her boss. "dale fortuna is in a coma. He got beat up pretty good by ingles' men. They must have thought he was dead; they dumped his body on a landfill site."

"jesus." Enver was shocked and unsurprised in equal measure. "how is he?"

"not good. Traumatic brain injury."

"fuck."

Lisa nodded. "yeah. There's something else. An attempt was made on harpa malhotra's life. She's okay, but pretty shaken up. Arlo's convinced harpa is suspicious."

Enver shook his head. "this isn't good. Look, we can't tell pad anything."

Lisa rocked back. "are you serious? You can't keep this from her, enver."

"i have to. If she finds out dale is in the hospital, she'll want to go back, and the second she lands on american soil, ingles will kill her."

Lisa put her hand on enver's arm. "calm down. Padme is a grown woman you cannot make this decision for her. This is her family."

Enver shook his head, his face set and grim. "no. At least, not yet. Give me some time to figure things out first."

Lisa sighed. "okay. But please, don't disrespect padme's choices for her own life. It's not like you."

Enver was still thinking about lisa's words as they sat down to supper. Padme had prepared a light and delicious fish curry for them and lisa swooned over the flavors. "i've been living on pizza for the last month. This is heaven." She smiled at her friend, who flushed at the praise.

"glad you like it. Can you stay for a while?"

"just a couple of days, but we'll have time to catch up."

Enver felt padme stroke his arm. "honey, you okay?"

He leaned over and kissed her cheek. "just fine, cara mia."

. . .

LATER, in bed, they made love more quietly than usual, not wanting to make lisa, who was sleeping in the next room, uncomfortable. Enver stroked the hair back from padme's lovely face as he thrust into her. Padme hitched her legs around his waist. "weird, being so quiet," she whispered, and they both chuckled. "i'm pretty sure the people on the other side of the island will wonder what's happened to us."

They both started to laugh then, and enver lost his rhythm and buried his face in her neck to muffle his laughter.

"hey, what did lisa say to you out on the beach? You came back, and your face was all stressed out."

Enver was glad his face was hidden. "just business stuff. A couple of takeover bids and i'm not there to oversee them, is all. Doesn't matter."

He felt bad for lying to padme, but he could not countenance her finding out about dale fortuna. She would demand they go back and even now, here, safe on the island, enver's nightmares about her being killed were tormenting him.

To his relief, padme didn't question him further, but the next morning when padme was still asleep, enver saw lisa jogging back along the beach and went out to meet her.

"listen," he said, "i want to know everything that's been going on back in the states since padme left. Everything."

Lisa sighed and nodded. "i was going to walk a couple of miles along the beach to cool down. Come walk with me."

PADME WAS AWAKE ONLY a few minutes after enver left the bed and she padded through the quiet house to find him. She saw him walking down the beach with lisa and shrugged. She went to grab a shower and get dressed, and as she was toweling her hair dry, she walked past lisa's room. Lisa's laptop sat on her bed. Padme stared at it for a long moment before going to check where enver was now. She saw them far down the beach. Dropping the towel, she scooted back to lisa's room and opened the laptop.

Opening a browser, she resisted the temptation to look up her family and friends or any news in seattle and instead concentrated on her immediate problem. She typed in "abortion in the maldives" into the search engine, then saw with a sinking heart that it was prohibited, and in any case, the spouse or significant other had to be informed.

"shit." She held her head in her hands for a moment, then slid a hand over her belly. This was real. It was happening. "it's not that i don't want you, little one," she said, her voice breaking. "it's that i can't want you right now." She sighed and scrubbed the browser history.

The weight of responsibility was crushing her and she needed some comfort. She gave into her worst instincts and googled severin, harpa, the forresters, and then finally, dale.

The shock was icy cold. Fbi agent found beaten, near death in city landfill. A photo of dale in his graduation uniform was under the headline. She read the whole article.

Only a year into his fledgling fbi career, agent dale fortuna, 33, was found almost beaten to death in a seattle landfill site. He was rushed to hospital, where he underwent a thirty-hour brain surgery to save his life and while doctors were successful, the tacoma native lies in a deep coma in a seattle hospital. Doctors say it is too soon to know if he will ever come out of it.

It's not the first time tragedy has touched the young agent. Just over eight months ago, his agency partner, padme kaur, was shot protecting shipping billionaire enver toscano as he gave evidence against the mighty ingles corporation. Miss kaur survived the attack despite being shot three times, but was recently herself the victim of a savage and as yet unsolved murder.

PADME WAS SHAKING, trembling so hard that when she stood to go to the bathroom to throw up, she slammed into the walls and doors as she staggered. She barely made it to the toilet before she threw up over and over again until there was nothing left. She sobbed out all her pain, every bit of emotion she'd been holding onto since before she came here, leaving her friends, her mom, the horror of being shot, the separation from enver ... who had lied to her. She knew without a doubt that the news about dale was what lisa had told enver yesterday—and he had kept it from her.

She cried for what seemed like hours, but when she felt enver's arms go around her she fought him off, screaming at him not to touch her, and ran from the house, passing a shocked lisa on her way out. She ran and ran down the beach.

Enver caught up with her, but she screamed at him to leave her alone and kept running before collapsing into the sand and gasping for air. Enver had lied to her. About something as big as this, about dale being nearly killed. What else was he keeping from her?

All she knew right now was that she had enver's child growing inside her and a lover who she didn't know if she could trust—and a best friend who was lying in a hospital bed because of her.

ENVER, shell-shocked, returned to the house to be greeted by lisa carrying her laptop. "enver, she used my laptop."

Enver felt his heart sink. Padme knew about dale.

16

CHAPTER SIXTEEN

Severin wondered at the sheer tragedy of it. Eight months ago, she was sitting by padme's hospital bed. Now she was here with dale. Another soul who had no one else in his life. She held dale's hand as she had padme's and willed him to survive.

"hey there." Henry jones pushed the door open. "the nurse told me you were with him. I thought i'd bring you some hot coffee and a danish."

Severin smiled at him. "you are a sweetheart, thank you." She took the coffee from him and sipped it.

Henry went to dale and placed his hand on his forehead. "how is he?"

"no change."

Henry shook his head. "god." He sat down opposite severin. "you visit often?"

"every day," she said softly, reaching out to take dale's hand again. "he doesn't have any one else." She smiled at henry. "sorry, i mean, apart from you."

"he and pad were like children to me. Both of them so brilliant and dedicated, even if padme chose a different path eventually."

"he's still alive," severin said softly, not looking at henry.

"what?"

She smiled a little reprovingly. "you said 'he and pad were like children to you.' dale is still alive."

"yes, of course. Sorry—a slip of the tongue." They sat in silence for a moment. "how are you dealing with padme's loss? I mean, is there anything i can do for you?"

Severin shook her head. "no." She debated whether to tell him her theory, that padme was alive, but she didn't want to put henry in a difficult position. Dale had been so adamant that they should keep it to themselves. "no, thank you, henry."

He stayed a little longer, but when she was alone, severin felt more at peace. She went to stand at the window, looking out over the city at night. Where are you, pad? Wherever you are, i hope you've found peace, safety, and love. I miss you. I love you.

Come home.

ENVER WAS SITTING in the living room with lisa with his head in his hands when padme came back. Her face was expressionless, but her whole body was tense. Enver knew not to touch her, as much as he might want to. He waited for padme to speak as she sat in the chair opposite him.

"i'm pregnant."

Enver felt a rush of joy, but seeing padme's pale, stern face, he had to once again restrain himself. "that's the best news, pad. I'm so happy."

Padme shook her head. "enver ... no. It isn't the best news, it's the worst. The very worst. We both have targets on our backs. Do you think i would put a child in danger like that?" She sighed, her shoulders slumping. "have you any idea how long i've dreamed of having your child? But i don't even know if i can trust you. Why didn't you tell me about dale?"

Enver sighed and rubbed his hands on his face. "because i know what you'll say."

"we have to go back."

He shook his head. "no."

Padme leaned forward in her chair, her eyes softening. "we have to finish this, enver. I won't live like this—i won't have our child brought into a world where he or she could lose us in a split second, or worse, be murdered. Lisa." She looked to the other woman, sitting silently at their side. "you must see this too?"

Lisa sighed. "i hate to agree but yes, i think it's the only way for you both to have a happy life."

Enver made a noise and felt both irritated and terrified. "and you don't think putting yourself back in ingles' sights will be riskier? Do you remember what he did to julia? It won't matter to him that you're pregnant; he'll cut our child right out of you."

Padme winced, but enver wasn't sorry. She had to know the risks. "what are you suggesting, pad? We kill ingles?"

She looked at him steadily without saying anything, and suddenly he knew exactly what she was saying. Yes. Kill frederick ingles. Without him, his family business would crumble, and they would be free.

"pad, even if we kill ingles, don't you think they'll seek revenge?"

"that's why you reach out first to ingles' enemies. You told me yourself that there are so many families waiting to take over from ingles that it won't matter about the rest of his family, what's left of it. They'll be so grateful we got rid of him, we'll have a worldwide network of protection."

Enver stared at his lover. "you really want to get into bed with these people?"

"of course not, and i'm not saying do business with them. Just make it clear that if we do this, then they owe us a life free from danger."

Lisa shrugged. "it could work. It's certainly no worse than hiding out here forever, waiting to be found."

"what about the men loyal to ingles?" Enver was starting to feel outnumbered by the women, and he didn't want to admit they might be right.

Lisa scoffed. "they're loyal to a paycheck, enver, not ingles. He treats them like shit."

Enver got up and paced around, thinking. "how would this work initially?"

"i call henry, get them to ease our passage back to seattle, get protection. Then we proceed with our 'comeback,' appearing in carefully stage-managed public areas where frederick ingles thinks he can get to us."

Enver looked at padme with a grim half-smile. "you've really thought this through, huh?"

She nodded. "ever since i found out i was pregnant. This has to end, enver. I want severin to know her grandchild and for him or her to play with cosima's kids. It's not just about you and me anymore."

Enver felt a wave of certainty come over him. They could do this—they could fight for the life they wanted. Padme was watching him.

"that house, that little house on the italian coast," she said softly, and he nodded.

"i want that too, cara mia. Okay. Okay, then. Let's hash this out before you call henry, and we'll get things moving. Let's go home, pad. Let's start our real lives together."

. . .

THREE HOURS LATER, padme waited nervously as she listened to the phone ring at the other end of the line. She smiled when she heard his warm voice. "henry ... it's me."

17

CHAPTER SEVENTEEN

One week later ...

DALE WAS HOVERING at the very edge of consciousness, having climbed from a chasm of darkness. He could hear the voices around him, the doctors and nurses, so he knew he wasn't dead. But still, he was so tired. His head throbbed with pain. He had felt a soft hand holding his, a gentle voice calling him out of the dark. Severin.

She wasn't in the room with him now, but as dale thought about opening his eyes for the first time, he heard the door creak open. Someone came into the room, but didn't say anything. He heard the faint dial tone as whoever it was placed a call.

"ingles, it's henry. Yeah, he's still in a coma. Listen, i thought you said you were going to end him. I can't have him waking up and interfering now; we're so close. Yeah. I know, fuck, ingles, she's coming back. She's coming back, and i'm giving you exactly what you wanted. She and toscano are delivering themselves to me in an hour. They're yours as soon as the money hits my account. Fine. Do it."

Dale was rigid with shock and horror. He was glad now he hadn't opened his eyes. He didn't want henry to know he had just discovered his duplicity. Henry would kill him without a second thought.

God ... henry? Kind, generous, grandfatherly henry? And now he was delivering padme into the arms of her killer. Dale couldn't believe it.

He felt henry lean over him and kept very still, not even moving his eyes under his closed lids.

"you shoulda just died, kid. It ain't gonna be pretty from now on," henry said softly. Dale held his breath until he heard the door close, then opened his eyes. His hand fumbled for the call button, and when the nurse arrived, he tried to speak.

"hold on, honey. Let me just wet your mouth."

He felt a blissful wetness on his lips. "severin," he said in barely a whisper. "please get severin now ..."

When severin rushed to his side, he stared up at her with pain-filled eyes and began to cry. "he's going to get her killed, sev. Oh god ... oh god ..."

HENRY WAS WAITING with a limousine on the tarmac at seatac as enver's private jet flew in. Padme knew enver was nervous. As they alighted from the plane, she saw his eyes raking the scene, looking for danger. She squeezed his hand. "stop. It'll be okay."

Henry hugged padme. "can't tell you how good it is to see you, padme."

She smiled at him. "you too, henry. Sorry we had to go through all that to get me out of the country."

"where were you, out of interest?"

Padme looked at enver, who cleared his throat. "we'd rather not say, henry. Just in case."

Henry smiled. "of course. Look, we have arranged a safe-house outside seattle. Pad, severin is waiting for you there."

Padme looked astonished and overwhelmed. "you told her?"

Henry shrugged. "she came to me, said she knew you were alive and that i had something to do with it. Something about the dna on the body we used. Anyhoo, i thought you could use another friendly face. Enver, your men are stationed along the route and are at the house. I'll be driving you there myself."

Enver was surprised. "you will?"

Henry gave him an expansive smile. "i just don't trust anyone else to do it."

He motioned for them to get into the limousine. Padme held enver's hand in the back of the car as they set off.

Severin. Soon she would see her mother again, and it should have filled her with joy, but something was off, and she couldn't pin down what it was. She looked at the back of henry's head. It was odd that he, the head of their field office, who was high up on the fbi ladder, would do something as menial as driving them to a safe house.

When she had spoken to him on the phone, he had agreed that coming home was best. "you can't run forever, pad."

He'd agreed so easily that something hadn't sat right with padme since, but this was henry she was talking about, her mentor, her guide.

Still, she had pushed forward with their plans and now they were heading to what padme hoped would only be a temporary home. Ingles must know they were back already; she didn't doubt that he had spies all over the airport. They had made the decision to fly back in enver's private plane and had filed a flight plan the day before. The wheels had been set in motion, and now they had to follow through.

Henry chatted happily, but neither enver nor padme felt like talking. It was dusk as they drove up to the small house henry had procured. Henry helped padme out of the car and she smiled her thanks. A shock ran through her when she noticed that henry's smile did not reach his eyes, and somehow, in that moment, she knew. She turned to speak to enver, to try and warn him, but henry clamped his hand over her mouth and dragged her toward the house as a gang of men rushed enver and overwhelmed him. He had no time to react.

Henry dragged a struggling padme into the house. "i'm sorry, pad, but it has to be this way."

Padme kicked and bit, but henry was too strong for her. He threw her to the floor of the living room, and she felt a hand under her chin as her face was tilted upwards. Frederick ingles smiled at her. "beautiful padme, how nice of you to join me for your actual murder."

Enver was dragged inside, and he, too, struggled against his captors. "motherfuckers! Figli di puttana!"

He saw henry jones come out of the living room. "you son of a bitch!"

Henry slammed his fist into enver's face. "mind your manners, asshole. Give mr. Ingles a little time to prepare miss kaur for her murder, then take this piece of shit in to watch."

Enver spat at henry, who ignored the gesture. "she trusted you," enver growled, beyond angry now. "how can you do this to her?"

"do what?" Henry asked. "she's already dead. I know because i read the eulogy at her funeral. What ingles does to her in there is none of my business."

He walked out, and enver struggled with his captors until they heard frederick ingles call out to them. "bring toscano in."

. . .

Enver, his mouth full of blood, went cold when he saw padme tied to a chair, her shirt torn open. Frederick gestured to the chair opposite her. "put him there. I want him to have a good seat to watch her bleed."

Padme met enver's eyes; they were full of sorrow. "i'm sorry," she said, "this is my fault."

"i love you," he said softly, but then screamed with rage and grief as frederick drove the knife halfway into padme's side. She gasped at the pain of it, not wanting to cry out or give frederick ingles the satisfaction. He looked pleased with himself anyway, wrenching the blade from her.

"finally," he breathed, as if the act of stabbing padme had released some kind of tension within him. He smiled at a raging, devastated enver. "as i told padme over and over, this was inevitable. Now, i'm going to enjoy this, as we take it slow."

"bastardo! She's pregnant, ingles, have some mercy!" Enver was hysterical in his grief. Blood was pouring from the wound on padme's side.

"oh, shut the fuck up, that was just a flesh wound." Ingles smirked. "this one, however, is going right in the center of her belly, all the way ... in."

"no!"

Smirking, frederick drew back his arm to stab padme again, but there was a sound of breaking glass and a small red dot appeared on frederick's face, just beneath his right eye. He looked confused for a second, then dropped like a stone, crumpling to the ground, his eyes open and staring. The blood began to trail down his face—the bullet had destroyed his brain. A sniper had taken him out. Finally, frederick ingles was dead.

Enver didn't hesitate. He lurched forward towards a bleeding padme and untied her from the chair, pulling her into his arms.

A second later, lisa, arlo forrester, and a troop of black-clothed operatives, all armed, burst into the room. Enver gaped at them all for a second, then turned his attention back to his lover.

Padme held her hand over her stab wound, pressing down, trying to keep the blood inside. Despite the shallowness of the wound, she was bleeding heavily. She looked up at him with frightened eyes. "the baby," she whispered. In that second, all that mattered to enver was getting his beloved padme to a hospital and saving their child and their future together.

18

CHAPTER EIGHTEEN

Dale was getting used to the wheelchair now, and so when no nurses were looking, he scooted down to padme's room. She was lying on top of her bed, looking bored, but grinned when she saw him.

"you'll get in trouble."

"i don't care," he said, grinning. "you look better."

Padme nodded. "much. It wasn't that deep, but they're keeping me for observation. The baby is fine though, little slugger that she is."

"it's a girl?"

Padme grinned. "i don't know that for sure; i just feel it. Anyway, how about you? You getting out of that thing anytime soon?"

Dale shrugged. "looks like. I have to say, i'm kind of sick of hospitals at the moment."

"i'll bet. Dale, look, i'm ..."

"if you say you're sorry one more time, pad, i will kick your ass. From this wheelchair."

"try it, bitch." But she grinned at him. Dale glanced around the room.

"where's enver? Thought you two were joined at the hip."

Padme laughed. "at the groin, actually."

"tmi."

She chuckled. "severin wrestled him into submission and made him go to her house for food, a shower, and some rest. God, it sounds so good to say that. So good to know we can now move freely around, be open, and it is heavenly."

"yeah, because it must have been so rough in the maldives," dale looked at her askance, and she grinned, acquiescing.

"it is paradise; i won't argue that. But you weren't there. My family is here, dale."

Dale smiled at her. "i had heard about a move to italy. We're not there, either."

"the difference being you could come visit us there whenever you wanted, doofus."

"i know."

They sat in companionable silence for a few minutes. "you haven't mentioned him," dale said.

Padme sighed. "henry? No. I don't even want to hear his name, never mind speak it or talk about him ever again."

"his trial will be something."

Padme nodded grimly. "bastard."

"yes."

Padme's expression cleared. "enough of him. The future is all that matters now."

Dale nodded. "you, enver, and the bean. You guys getting married?"

Padme shrugged. "he hasn't asked me."

"you should ask him. The sisterhood might forgive you then."

Padme grinned. "in all truth, i'm honestly not bothered about being married. I want to be with enver for all time. A piece of paper isn't going to change that."

. . .

Later, when enver returned, looking refreshed and relaxed for the first time in weeks, padme kissed him hello. "docs say they're letting me out tomorrow."

Enver smiled, pulling her against him. "good. I'm ready for our life to begin, pad, at last.

She gazed up at this remarkable man that she had given up everything for, had nearly died for—twice—and nodded, her eyes shining. "at last, my love. At long last."

Three months later ...

His lips trailed along the length of her spine until they rested against the back of her neck. "are you ready for me, il mia amore?"

He pushed her thick dark hair away from her face as she nodded and gently, he parted her legs and thrust his rampant cock into her swollen, wet cunt. Padme gasped, her face turning towards him so he could kiss her as they fucked, his hands pinning hers to the bed.

Outside, the sea rushed against the cliffs of the italian coast, the sun pelted down, heating the ground. Enver braced himself as he began to fuck her harder and deeper and longer until she was crying his name out again and again. He came hard, groaning, telling her again and again how much he loved her.

Afterward, they lay, wrapped in each other's arms, enver's hand splayed across the small bump in her belly. And now they knew—a girl ... and a boy. Twins. They hadn't expected it, but it had been a source of great joy to them when they found out.

Padme had found the house by accident, randomly browsing

properties on an italian website, but when she saw it, she knew she had found their home. It was a huge, recently renovated farmhouse with an indoor pool, and plenty of space for their children to run and play and be free. Enver had agreed, and the sale had gone through within a few days.

They had been here for a month now, and in padme's heart, she knew she had found her place in the world.

She looked at her lover now and smiled at him. "ti amo, enver toscano."

He grinned and kissed her. "ti amo, padme." He picked up her left hand and traced a circle around her third finger. "sposami?" He asked in a soft, almost nervous voice, because they'd talked about it, but not seriously.

Now, though, and despite what she'd told dale, padme looked into the glorious green eyes of the man she loved and could only think of one thing she wanted to say.

"si, enver, si, si, si ..."

THE END

SIGN UP TO RECEIVE FREE BOOKS

Sign Up to Receive Free E-Books and Audiobook Codes.

Would you like to read **The Unexpected Nanny, Dirty Little Virgin** and **other romance books** for **free**?

You can sign up to receive these free e-books and audiobooks by typing this link into your browser:

https://www.steamyromance.info/free-books-and-audiobooks-hot-and-steamy/

Or this one:

https://www.steamyromance.info/the-unexpected-nanny-free/

PREVIEW OF THE MIDNIGHT CLUB

By Michelle Love

Blurb

Maceo Bartoli. Alex Milland. Lisander Duarte. Benoit Vaux. Seth Cantor. They are five of the most eligible billionaires on the planet— and they share a strange coincidence. All five were born at midnight on the same day in the same year. Friends and playboys all, they call themselves The Midnight Club and they have only one rule: to never let a woman come between them. But as they grow older, this rule becomes harder and harder to keep. And when they meet the women who could change their lives forever, they realize that it's time for the Club to mature.

Despite the recent murder of Viola, Alex's fiancée, the friends don't know that any woman they meet from now on could also be in terrible danger. Because someone wants to keep The Midnight Club exclusive and will stop at nothing to do it. Does the threat come from outside, or is one of The Midnight Club a vicious and merciless killer?

DUSK - MIDNIGHT CLUB PART 1

She was tied to the chair, shivering and terrified but determined not to show him how scared she was. He'd stripped her down to her underwear now, and his hands roamed freely over her skin.

"So soft," he cooed in a sing-song voice, almost tender. She could almost believe him to be that caring—if it wasn't for the crossbow in his other hand. He saw her looking at him and grinned. He brought it up and leveled it at her. Point blank.

"Tell me you love me," he said tenderly, and she looked him straight in the eye.

"No." Her voice was strong. Defiant.

He smiled. "What a waste of such beauty," he said and fired the bolt deep into her body.

The pain was unimaginable ...

Venice, Italy, March 14, a year previously...

Alex Milland was the first to arrive in *The Floating City Galleria* and immediately he went to find Maceo. The art gallery may have been small, but its position overlooking the lagoon afforded wonderful views across the city. One whole wall was glass; the rest of the walls were painted a stark white. The effect was to make the works of art hanging on them stand out. It worked.

ALEX NODDED TO HIMSELF APPROVINGLY. He smiled to himself as he noticed a few harassed-looking but very attractive assistants scuttling around. He wondered how many of them Maceo was fucking. *Dumb question,* he said to himself. Maceo would have screwed them *all* at their first interview.

Maceo himself was in his office on the third floor. Alex knocked on the door and didn't wait for an answer. Maceo looked up and grinned.

"Alex, how good to see you." He got up and the two men bear hugged. Maceo, his green eyes a contrast to his dark curls and swarthy skin, studied his friend. "How are you? Really?'

Alex sighed inwardly. He would be getting this question a lot today. "I'm fine, Maceo. It's been months since Viola died and, not that I will ever get over it, but I have to try and function. So I need this. I need to celebrate something good. The place looks incredible.'

Maceo nodded, grinning. Humility wasn't in Maceo's playbook. "Thanks, Alex. I admit, it does look spectacular. And you should see who we have exhibiting at the moment." He rattled off a few names, and Alex was impressed. Some of the biggest names in modern art—he had to admire Maceo's work ethic. He doubted anyone said no to the young man in front of him.

Young man. Alex shook his head, smiling. He and Maceo

were the exact same age; Alex just felt like the grandad of their group. The club. The Midnight Club. In truth, he had always considered himself the oldest of them—except for maybe Seth. But then again, he and Seth were as close as twins. Maceo was the young puppy of the group— passionate, confident, a visionary.

Maceo gathered up a pile of papers and yelled, "Lucia!" A gorgeous blonde girl walked in and Alex smiled at her. She nodded back, friendly but professional.

"You have an intercom, Maceo. Don't scream at me," she snapped at Maceo, who grinned unrepentantly. She took the papers from him and, as she was walking away, she looked back over her shoulder. "I have to duck out for a couple of hours. Personal errand. Your other friends are waiting downstairs."

Maceo hooted his delight. "Good! Come, Alex, let's go see them." And he bore his friend away back down the main gallery.

ORIANTHI ROY STOOD outside the airport arrivals, feeling lost. Lucia was late, and Ori wondered if she should hail a cab. Italy was new to her, and the flight had tired her out. Now she felt discombobulated as people pushed passed her, meeting their loved ones, loudly talking, and yelling everywhere.

"This was meant to be a break. A *quiet* break," she muttered to herself, then felt a flood of relief as she saw Lucia waving at her. Her friend hugged her.

"God, I'm sorry, Ori. The traffic was insane. Is that your case? Come on, I'll get you settled at home."

Lucia drove them back into the city. Ori was surprised. "I thought it was all canals?"

Lucia grinned. "Not yet. We're still on the mainland. Listen, I have to tell you, my boss is having his grand gallery opening tonight and so I have to work. But I have arranged for you to be on the guest list—don't worry, it's an invite-only thing and won't go too late. But I would really like you to come."

Damn it, Ori thought, but kept a smile on her face. "Love to, Luce. Listen, I can't thank you enough for letting me stay. I just needed to get away from all the craziness back home."

Lucia looked at her with sympathy. "I knew it was bad, Ori, but I have to tell you, you scared me when you called me the other night. What has Janek done now?"

Ori felt sick at the mere mention of his name—Tyson Janek III, congressman and her stepfather. Recently outed by the mainstream press as screwing a lot of his colleagues' wives, he had been forced to step down, but even now was working to retake his position. The fact that he was doing it by calling in favors from people who were less than respectable didn't matter to Tyson Janek. He didn't care who he stepped on or who he destroyed. When he had married Ori's mother, Ori had been ten years old and in deep mourning for the father she had lost. Ori's mother, Kathryn, after being disinherited from her father's newspaper fortune , had married the charming and handsome Tyson and had given birth to Ori's younger half-brother, AJ soon after. AJ was the best and only good thing about the marriage, as far as Ori was concerned.

Almost as soon as Tyson had married her mother, he started to abuse Ori. At first, it was insidious—the odd touch here and there that could be explained away. But on the night of her twelfth birthday, her mother was asleep when Tyson came into Ori's room. That night he raped her for the first time. That night he threatened the life of her mother, her baby brother, and Ori herself for the first time. It didn't stop until Ori left for college. She never returned home. Tyson persuaded her mother to write Ori out of her will, leaving her penniless.

Determined not to take a penny from Tyson or touch the small amount of money her mother had left AJ, Ori worked in retail stores, bars, restaurants, diners, all to make enough to pay her rent and keep food on the table. At college, she excelled and graduated from her arts program with honors. It was only when she started to be offered places in graduate programs that Tyson started to interfere again. Suddenly Ori would be turned down or rejected for places she had initially been offered unconditionally. Tyson broke into her apartment one night and told her that she would never be free of him, that she belonged to him. When her mother died five years ago, Ori had taken the still-teenage AJ and moved away from New York, hiding out in Arizona, and putting AJ through state school.

Tyson had found them within weeks and, threatening Ori with arrest, had taken his son back to New York. Unwilling to leave AJ, Ori had reluctantly followed, knowing that as long as AJ was underage, Tyson had them.

He raped her again on her twenty-fifth birthday, and this time, he beat her too. Leaving her bleeding and bruised, he got dressed and grabbed her by the throat. "Try and leave me, Ori. Just try. They won't be able to identify your body for weeks."

But living in a world of terror can make the strongest person break. Ori quit her job and stayed at home for three months, not speaking to anyone. In the end, it took a concerned ex-co-worker to come find her and pull her out of the mire. Lucia had been over from Italy to see her parents, Italian immigrants to New York, and had been horrified to see Ori so depressed. She had told her then to come to Italy, to escape.

Three years after that final rape, when Tyson's scandal erupted and the press was all over their family, AJ checked himself into a facility for depression, and Ori called Lucia. It had been her one chance to escape Tyson. Now that she knew AJ was okay and that he was safe where he was ...it was time for her to look out herself.

"Hey, penny for them. We're here." Lucia nudged her,

smiling.

Lucia's apartment was huge. Her guest bedroom looked out over a canal and had a little balcony where Ori could sit and sketch or just sit and watch the day. She looked around the bedroom. Huge bed, vanity, en-suite bathroom. A small table and chair for her to work at. Ori smiled at Lucia gratefully.

"Luce, this is amazing, thank you"

Lucia hugged her. "I hoped you'd like it. Now, everything is handled. I've even taken the liberty of getting you a few clothes. Now, I know you hate dressing up, but believe me, try it, just for an evening. I've bought you plenty of jeans and T-shirts too"

Ori laughed. "I don't know how to thank you, Luce"

"I want you to relax. Be yourself. Don't worry about money or anything. I have too much as it is. Maceo's a shit, but he pays exceptionally well"

Ori was curious about her friend's boss. "Why is he a shit?"

Lucia chuckled, rolling her eyes. "Don't get me wrong. I like him a lot, but he's a whore. A complete and utter man-slut. He's already worked his way around my staff"

"You?"

"Hell, no. I've had my fill of Maceo's kind – I'm happy with my boyfriend. And get this: Maceo has four friends, all gorgeous, all billionaires. All of them exactly like him" She told Ori about The Midnight Club and Ori laughed.

"Cavemen?"

"Some of them. A couple of them are okay ... Seth and Alex. Alex just lost his fiancée a few months ago. He's a wreck, but trying not to show it. Anyway, you'll meet them tonight, no doubt"

LUCIA LEFT her alone to rest, and Ori walked slowly around the room, feeling the soft white voile curtains and the firm mattress of the bed. She curled up on it now, phone in hand. AJ had messaged her.

How's Italia, sis?

She smiled. *Beautiful, but wish you were here too.*

She checked the clock. A quarter of two. She wondered if AJ would be in one of his group meetings about now. She didn't hear back from him, so she assumed he was and closed her eyes. Just five minutes' sleep. Within minutes she was dead to the world as, outside her window, Venice basked in the early afternoon sun.

MACEO BARTOLI SAID a few words at the beginning of the reception. Then, with a flourish, he cut the ribbon and the gallery was open. He felt a certain pride as his guests chattered excitedly and sought him out to ask questions. He especially enjoyed the attentions of the beautiful women who drifted around the room. He glanced up and saw his four best friends huddled against the back wall, grinning at his easy flirtation with the guests. He managed to make his way over to them and gratefully took a glass of champagne from Seth, the tall Canadian.

"Dude, congratulations. A triumph"

Maceo raised his glass. "To us"

Lisander, the brooding Argentinian fashion designer, nodded at some of the exhibits. "Nice showing of South American art. Thank you, Maceo"

Maceo grinned. "If I could only persuade you to allow me to hang some your design sketches, Sander"

Benoit, an elegant Frenchman, flicked his dark brown eyes across the room. An architect, he nodded approvingly at the galleries design. "This is a good space, Maceo. A very good space"

Maceo grinned at him, his green eyes shining. "Enough about that." he raised his glass. "Happy birthday, my brothers"

LATER, he was talking to a local artist, assuring the man that he would champion Italian art above all else. The man, although talented, had god awful dog breath and so Maceo was edging away from him slowly. Finally, with a sigh of relief, he managed to escape to one of the balconies. He stepped out into the cool Venetian air and heaved a sigh of relief. He didn't see the young woman sitting on one of the stone plinths until she gave a small, embarrassed cough. He turned to see a small brunette in a dark mauve cocktail dress. She had long dark brown hair pulled over one shoulder and her cheeks were adorably flushed pink.

"I'm sorry. I didn't mean to startle you"

She was American, with a soft, melodic voice and eyes the color of the ocean, dark green and large. She had thick, thick dark lashes and a rosebud mouth. Maceo felt his cock twitch and he immediately went into seduction mode. He'd exhausted his supply of assistants, and he was damned if he was going to sleep alone tonight. He ran his eyes over her body, taking in the curve of her waist, full breasts, and shapely legs. He could already imagine that lush pink mouth around his cock. He smiled at the young woman.

"It is my pleasure, Miss …?"

She looked wary. "Orianthi"

"Miss Orianthi"

"No." She chuckled slightly, "That's my first name"

"It's beautiful," he said without missing a beat, his eyes locked on hers, and holding out his hand. She shook it. "Maceo Bartoli. Did you like the exhibit?"

"Very much. You have a Hopper on loan, I see. He's my hero. I also liked the *Mamani Mamani* selection"

Maceo's eyebrows shot up. "You know your paintings"

Ori nodded. "I majored in art and I worked for a while as a curator"

Maceo was impressed, but he was still distracted by her body. He could smell her scent— perfume, soap, clean laundry and fresh air. He wondered how her cunt would taste and how it would feel. He shot a quick look in through the French windows … could he take her here? Suddenly being inside this beautiful woman was all he could think about.

He blinked, trying to concentrate on what she was saying. He smiled as she stammered to a halt, suddenly noticing his scrutiny. "Orianthi, would you care to have a late supper with me tonight?"

She grinned, and her smile made his cock thicken painfully. She really was gorgeous. But she shook her head. "Mr. Bartoli, I should tell you. I'm staying with Lucia Fernando. She and I are best friends and let's just say … your reputation precedes you. Thank you, but no"

She nodded, half-smiling, and went back inside, leaving Maceo staring after her. *Remind me to fire Lucia,* he thought to himself, knowing that a) he would do nothing of the sort; he couldn't function without Lucia running his business and b) … that whoever she was, the girl called Orianthi had just laid down the ultimate challenge to Maceo Bartoli. *Get her into bed or die trying.* Maceo grinned to himself and went back into the gallery to rejoin his friends.

THEY SAY the first time is the hardest. They say it gets easier the more you kill. Yes, he had found that to be true. Killing Viola had been life-changing, along with that surprise in her eyes as he shot the crossbow bolt into her at point blank range and the horror. Then there was her blood, carrying her lifeless body to the edge of the river and dumping her in, watching her blood mix with the water. He had never felt such peace.

And now he knew he would do the same to any woman that the Midnight Club grew attached to or fell in love with. He would kill them all. He stared at the girl in the mauve dress. She looked like Viola too— dark, sensual, curvy. He hoped she would stay away from the Club and away from them all. Otherwise ... it would be her death sentence.

ALEX MILLAND ROLLED over onto his back and sighed. No sleep again. Three a.m. He considered, then grabbed his phone. He knew one of his friends would still be up—well, he knew Maceo would also be up and fucking some hot girl he'd picked up at the opening. Alex grinned to himself. Maceo was a machine. He could turn his feelings off. Maceo was an expert at that, and Alex envied him for it.

No, he could call on Seth, the calm center of their group. Quiet, fiercely intelligent, and with an empathy that somehow the rest of them lacked, Seth was Vancouver's answer to Bill Gates. He was a brilliant mind but, Alex knew, also a solitary one. And, to Alex's own benefit tonight, Seth was also an insomniac. He sent Seth a text message, and sure enough, a reply came back almost immediately.

Bar is still open.

He found Seth sitting at the bar, nursing a glass of scotch. He looked exhausted, but smiled at his friend, sliding a bottle of Johnny Walker Blue over to him. "How're you doing, Alex?"

Alex shrugged. "Existing"

Seth nodded in sympathy. "I'm sorry, man. I can't even imagine. They still haven't a clue who murdered Viola?"

Alex sighed. "No. I can't get my head around it, Seth. I just don't get it. I just don't know what it would take for someone to do that to Viola, man. She was kind and loving to everyone. Such a fucking waste"

"I hear you, brother"

Alex took a slug of scotch. "I tell you, man, never again. No more long-term things. I don't think my heart could cope"

Seth studied him. "Alex ... you can't let this stop you from being happy ever again"

Alex gave a humorless laugh. "Look who's talking"

"That's different,' Seth said shortly. "Irina cheated on me. Not the same at all. I just haven't the time for relationships. I can get a quick fuck whenever I need it; why bother with the rest?"

"Cold"

"Not cold; smart"

Alex sighed. "Where are the others?"

"Not being smart"

Alex chortled. "God, you really did get up on the wrong side of the bed today"

Seth rubbed his face. "I just want some damn sleep, man"

"I know how you feel"

Seth put his arm around Alex's shoulders. "I'm sorry, buddy. You must miss her. We all do"

An hour later Alex was back in bed, listening to the rain fall outside. He closed his eyes, but he could only see Viola's pale, gray face. Dead. Her body so still on the mortuary slab. The detective asking him to identify her.

Alex pushed the thought away and finally, rolled over at six a.m., falling asleep.

Ori stood under the spray of the shower, trying to shake the dream she had just awoken from. Not that it was a nightmare—

far from it—and it was a change to have such a pleasant dreams for once. *Ha,* she thought. *Pleasant' is hardly the word. Try hot. Try sensual. Try the sexiest, most erotic dream she'd ever had.*

And of course, it had to be about that damn Maceo Bartoli, didn't it?

Ori closed her eyes and the water poured over her body. For a second she indulged in the remembrance of the dream ... the part where Maceo Bartoli ordered everyone out of his gallery except her, then made her stand naked in the middle of the floor while he circled her, watching, studying her, and describing everything he wanted to do to her. God, she shivered as she remembered, her hand snaking down her thigh and into her sex, rubbing her clit as she thought of him ordering her to spread her legs before he took out his enormously hard cock and ...

"Ori?" Lucia yelled through her bathroom door.

Ori's eyes snapped open and, flushing guiltily, she shut off the water and stepped out of the shower. Wrapping a towel around herself, she opened her bedroom door. Lucia looked apologetic.

"Hey, sweetie, I'm sorry. Maceo's called me into work, so we'll have to postpone our shopping trip"

Ori was disappointed. "Oh. Well, that's okay, I can just wander around and get to know the place. We can shop another day"

Lucia smiled at her gratefully. "Thanks, darling, I *am* sorry. Look, I have a handy travel guide book that I've left on the table—it was invaluable when I first moved here. Just be vigilant. OH, look what I'm saying. Is there a place in the world where we women don't have to be vigilant?"

Ori laughed. "Can't think of anywhere, but yes, I will be. I'll keep to the tourist traps"

. . .

AFTER HER FRIEND HAD GONE, Ori dressed in jeans and a loose, flowing white shirt. She pulled her long dark hair into a messy ponytail. Sliding her feet into her old battered Chuck Taylor's, she grabbed her bag, shoved the guidebook inside, and headed out.

This year, Venice in March was unseasonably warm, and soon Ori had lost herself in exploring the place, taking water taxis, letting herself drift down small passages. She ended up on the island of Giudecca and found a small bar-trattoria to have lunch in. She ordered a small tuna salad and ate with pleasure, a glass of wine on the table, watching the people as they passed on the street. She got lost in daydreaming, so when the man who appeared by her side spoke, she started in her chair.

Maceo Bartoli was smiling down at her and *god*, if a beat didn't start pulsing between her legs. He was gorgeous, all scruffy charm and confidence and very, very tempting, but Ori knew his type. Once he'd had her, she would be old news, and she didn't think her confidence could take that kind of hit right now.

"I'm sorry,' she said, coolly, "I didn't hear what you said"

Without being asked, Maceo sat down in the chair opposite her and signaled to the waiter. "I said, if I pretend that you agreed to have dinner with me, I can count this as our first date"

She glared at him. "Did you follow me?"

Maceo laughed. *God,* his smile really was something else ... *no. Do not fall for it,* she told herself sharply.

"I wish I were that sneaky," Maceo admitted. "But no, I promise. Coincidence. A happy one for me, at least. You?"

Ori hid a smile behind her wine glass. She had to admit his confidence was amusing. And being flirted with by a stunningly handsome man? *Not too shabby.* But she'd be damned if she'd let *him* know that. "I haven't made my mind up yet"

He laughed again, and something fluttered in her belly.

Maceo took out a cigarette pack, offered her one, and when she declined, stuck one in his mouth and lit it. He blew out a lungful of smoke—away from her, she noticed with gratitude. He was studying her.

"Tell me, Orianthi—"

"Ori. Just call me Ori"

He inclined his head gracefully. "Tell me, Ori. What are you doing in my city?"

She hesitated only a beat. "I'm taking a vacation. A sabbatical"

"Are you working?"

"Not currently" Why did that always make her feel like a waste of space?

Maceo did not seem fazed. "I think sometimes we need to take stock and reevaluate. A sabbatical is good"

Ori blinked. What was his game? Agreeing with her about everything? She narrowed her eyes at him. "Are you making fun of me?"

"Quite the contrary. I, myself, am a workaholic. I love the adrenaline rush, but I too have thought about taking an extended break"

Ori smiled at him. "And what would you do, Mr. Bartoli, on your break?"

He smiled. "I would dedicate myself to finding out the best way to fuck you, Ms. Roy. What you liked, what you didn't. I'd use my hands and my tongue to pleasure you until you screamed my name loud enough for the whole of Venice to hear. Then, just when you thought you couldn't take anymore, I would drive my cock deep inside you until you begged me to stop"

Ori, her breath caught in her chest, stared at him. *What the hell?* Was he serious? However angry she felt was belied by the fact she could feel herself getting wet as he spoke, wanting him to take her there, who cared who saw, *just fuck me, please* ...

Instead, she pulled herself together. "I imagine that there are some women upon whom that honesty would work,' she said rather primly, gathering her bag and scrabbling around for some cash to pay for her lunch. "I, however, am not one of them. Goodbye, Mr. Bartoli"

Leaving him grinning after her, she stalked off and caught a water taxi back to Lucia's house. *Of all the insufferable, egotistical assholes ...* She stomped into her room and flung her bag against the wall.

Yeah, but you can't help thinking about him, can you?

"Shut up," she told herself. God, she needed a distraction. She grabbed her phone and went to sit on the little balcony. She found the number of AJ's facility and waited. After a moment, the receptionist answered, and soon AJ was saying hello. His voice sounded dull.

"Hey, Boo," Ori said gently, knowing her brother's moods were erratic.

"Hey, funny face," he said and sighed. "It's good to hear from you. When are you coming back?"

Ori's heart twisted. "Sweetie, I—"

"No, sorry, don't answer that. I don't want you to come back yet, I'm sorry. I'm just a little down today"

"Have you been taking your meds?"

"Like I promised, sis. You heard from Dad?"

Ori grimaced. "No. Not a word"

"Have you seen the latest then? On the news? Some more women are coming forward. Seems Papa really can't keep it in his pants"

AJ's voice was so dead, flat, and lifeless Ori could have cried. That his father didn't give a crap about Ori was one thing—that he ignored his only child was unforgivable. 'Look, Boo, I can come back whenever and bust you out of there" She tried to make a joke out of it, and she heard AJ give a soft chuckle.

"You know, sis? Here was a good idea. This place, I mean. It is helping, obviously, some days more than others—but I do feel at last like I'm getting my head clear"

Ori gave a sigh of relief. "That is good news. Look, when I come back, we're going to go someplace where he can't touch us. I promise"

"That sounds like a plan"

WHEN SHE ENDED THE CALL, she felt calmer. AJ was making progress, and that was all that mattered now. Her younger half-brother was the love of her life, and she knew she would do anything to protect him. When he'd been diagnosed as having bipolar disorder at fourteen, Ori had been beside herself, terrified that he would kill himself with drugs or alcohol. Pinegap Rehabilitation Center was only the latest in a long chain of rehab places, but he seemed to be thriving there—most days. She hoped Tyson would stay away.

Just keep paying the bills and leave him alone, she thought to herself now. She considered, and then burrowed in her bag for her other phone, the one whose number Tyson would call her on. She kept it mostly off, unless AJ was unreachable. Then she turned it on in case of emergency.

Out of sheer masochism, she turned it on now. Her voicemail was full. Cursing herself, she listening to a few of the messages, all from Tyson. Some of them were rants about her disloyalty; others were disgustingly lewd. The latest were short and sweet. "Where the *fuck* are you, Orianthi? Do you think you can hide from me?"

She deleted every last one of them and then cursed. Why did she do that? It was evidence. "Dumb, stupid girl," she snarled at herself, then stopped. *Evidence.* Was she that convinced that one day she would *need* evidence against him? Fuck, she was messed up.

She pushed the thought away and went to make some dinner for Lucia. She had bought fresh ingredients for seafood linguine, and as she cooked, she could feel all the tension leach out of her. She chopped, diced, and steamed, and by the time Lucia got home from work, there were two plates piled high with pasta. Lucia swooned over the hot, buttery food, garlicky ciabatta on the side to soak up the creamy sauce.

"You are wasted as an art curator," Lucia told Ori afterward when they sat outside on the balcony with a half-empty bottle of wine between them. "You should retrain as a chef"

"Ha." Ori smiled, "One good dish doesn't make a chef"

They chatted easily and then Ori, not being able to help herself from talking about him, mentioned she had seen Maceo out on one of the islands. Lucia rolled her eyes.

"I wondered where he'd gotten to. I had buyers waiting. He seemed very pleased with himself when he got back. I hope it wasn't awkward"

"Not at all. You're right, though. He's trouble with a capital 'T'"

"Big, big trouble," Lucia agreed, then stared at her. "Oh god, you haven't got a crush, have you? Because he'll trample all over your heart if you let him"

"Don't be ridiculous, I don't know the man"

"Who needs to know a man when he looks like Maceo?"

"Sounds like I'm not the one with the crush" Ori chuckled at her friend's horror-stricken face.

"That is not what I meant, Orianthi, and you know it. But I'm not blind, I can see that the man is delicious. He's just too sure of himself"

Ori tapped Lucia's wineglass with her own. "That's what I think"

BUT LATER, in bed, she allowed herself to fantasize about what it would be like to be fucked by such a man. She imagined his lips against hers, her hand sliding down to his groin, feeling the hot length of his cock through the fabric of his pants, his fingers pulling at her panties, his cock gliding into her. Ori couldn't help rubbing her clit, imagining it was his tongue lashing around it, and she dreamed herself to orgasm, burying her face in her pillow to muffle her cries.

Just like every time she came though, afterward the tears would come, the release of tension too much for her, and she sobbed quietly until she fell into an uneasy sleep.

"YOU'RE STILL HERE"

Alex was surprised. Benoit and Lisander had already flown home to Paris and Buenos Aires respectively, but Alex had stayed to hang out with Maceo. Now he saw that Seth was at the table too. The tall Canadian smiled at him.

"I was persuaded to stay another night," he said, nodding at a grinning Maceo.

"Just one more quiet meal with friends," Maceo explained. "But sadly, Ben and Sander had to work. The never-ending toil," he said dramatically, and the other two laughed. Maceo was undoubtedly the joker of their group, but Alex knew that sometimes his friends, the stoic Ben especially, found him a little too much.

Tonight, however, he was in good form. "I must tell you, friends. I believe I have finally met my match"

"Ha," Seth snorted. "I'll believe it when I see it"

"No, no, really. This girl is special"

"They all are until you fuck them,' Alex said dryly.

Maceo threw up his hands, but laughed. "You have a fair point, my friend, but no. This one ... she has something else. She will not be so easily *had*"

"Oh, she *is* different," Seth nodded sagely. "... she has *taste*"

Maceo laughed, taking the ribbing in good heart. All three friends enjoyed the meal, joking and laughing. It wasn't until they were leaving the restaurant that the conversation turned serious.

Maceo looked at Alex steadily. "Alex, my brother ... will you be okay? Seth told me this morning that the *figlio di puttana* who killed Viola is still out there?"

Alex nodded, his eyes clouding over. "A part of me wants to find him first, so I can end this the way Viola deserves ... "

He gathered himself as his two friends looked at him sympathetically. "I'm sorry, guys. I'll get to the bottom of it, I swear I will"

LATER, Maceo himself drove both Alex and Seth to the airport. Hugging them goodbye, he made them a promise. "We will meet soon, again, yes?"

As he made his way back to the car, his attention was caught by a man in a long dark coat and sunglasses getting into a long black limousine. Sunglasses at night?

Maceo grinned to himself. "What are *you* hiding from?" He soon forgot about the man, channeling his thoughts more pleasurably into his latest project. *Orianthi Roy*. He could not stop thinking about her, to the point where he had actually called Lucia into his office earlier that day and asked her about her friend.

"You leave that girl alone," Lucia had said immediately. "She is not one of your conquests"

Maceo grinned now. *No. Not yet.* But he hadn't said that to Lucia. Out of all his colleagues, she was the one he was actually wary of—probably because she was amazing at her job and had turned him down flat when he'd tried his usual shtick on her first day at the gallery.

"That," she had said bluntly, grabbing his cock through his jeans, "isn't going to get anywhere near me. It does not interest me. Now—" she had released him. "Can we get back to work?"

Maceo laughed out loud now. He honestly could not imagine his business without Lucia. So could he risk her friendship just for the sake of fucking Orianthi?

For once, Maceo knew he would have to tread very, very carefully. If only he could stop thinking about Ori's lush curves or her pink, warm mouth ...

"ARE you sure you're going to be okay? I can always tell Johnny I can't make it this weekend"

Ori rolled her eyes at her friend. Lucia's boyfriend, a racecar driver, had called at the last minute, asking Lucia to fly to Monaco to see him. Ori could tell she was excited. "I'll be fine as long as you don't mind me pretending that this amazing place is my own for a week"

Lucia laughed. "Not at all. I know you, Miss Homemaker. I'll come back to brand new drapes and exquisitely crafted baked goods like in college. God, doesn't that seem a million years ago?"

"It does" Ori followed Lucia into her bedroom and sat on the bed while she packed. "I found this great little café today, overlooking the lagoon. It's quiet, and I can write there. Lucia, this city is growing on me, I have to say. As well as the obvious beauty of the place, I like the people and the serenity"

"Ha." Lucia snorted from the depths of her closet, "Wait until it's *Carnevale* time. Then you'll change your mind" She dragged a huge suitcase out of her closet and opened it. "Eww, is that a mouse?"

Ori peered in. "No, it's half an ear muff, you loon" She threw it at a relieved Lucia. "How's the Bartoli Bonefest going to cope without you for a week? Rich boy's going to have to get his own coffee"

Ori grinned at her friend as Lucia tried to look disapproving. "You are so mean"

"Haven't you been the one to warn me away from him?"

"Just because I don't want a nice girl like you to get hurt by Maceo doesn't mean I'm not very fond of him. Under all the bullshit ... well, let's just say I think still waters run deep"

Ori was surprised, but didn't say anything else. She'd spent the past few nights dreaming of Maceo Bartoli; if nothing else, he helped the nightmares stay away.

Lucia left a couple of hours later, with hugs and kisses and promises to call. And then Ori was truly alone. She felt weird banging around in the big apartment by herself and, since it was too early to call AJ, she decided to take her computer and go do some writing.

She went to the small café she had discovered and ordered coffee and gelato. Opening her computer, she launched her browser and checked the news in the States. Her stepfather was front page news again. Ori ignored the gnawing terror that Tyson Janek's handsome face gave her every time she saw it, and read through the story. More women coming forward with sexual assault claims. God, the man was a monster. Her eyes scanned the rest of the story, stopping when she saw her name mentioned.

"There are few people in this world whom I trust," Janek told a press conference, "but I know I can count on the support of my daugh-

ter, Orianthi, and my son, Adam James. They are the closest people to me" The congressman appeared emotional. *"I love them with all my heart; they truly are the best of me."*

"*Motherfucker ...*" Ori whispered to herself. God, he really was repellent. How much would it shock the world now to find out he was a rapist scumbag? Janek was entirely responsible for AJ's staggering lack of confidence and his depression. Ori was angrier for AJ than for herself—AJ was Janek's biological son, for chrissakes. She slammed the lid of her laptop down—a little too hard—and took a deep breath in. *AJ is safe and well away from him and so are you, Orianthi. So are you.*

She finished her coffee and settled down to work on her project. It was near dusk when she looked up from her work. She stretched and packed up her stuff. *Home, a bath, food, and a good book. Sounds like the perfect evening.* She was smiling to herself as she walked back slowly through the city. Her cell phone rang just as she reached the apartment. Lucia.

"Sweetie, I'm so sorry to ask you this," Lucia sounded panicked, "but Maceo is having a meltdown. One of his customers is saying a painting Maceo sold him is fake. Is there any chance you could go the gallery and help him out?"

Ori saw her perfect evening go up in smoke. "Of course, honey. Don't panic. I'm not a hundred percent sure what I can do though. I'm not an expert ...'

"That's the thing ... Ori, we have this happen to us all the time, and when it does, I usually act the part of the art expert. Most of the time it works, and we don't have to fly our real expert in from Geneva. So, if you could, you know, pretend ..."

Ori started to laugh. "You are kidding me, right?"

Lucia chuckled. "I wish I was"

Ori sighed. "No problem. Look, if I'm going to look the part, can I borrow your work clothes? I can't show up in jeans"

"Of course, anything you need. Thanks, Ori, I owe you one"

. . .

That was how, forty-five minutes later, Ori, dressed in a black skirt and jacket with her hair pulled back into a severe bun and her spectacles perched on her nose, marched into Maceo Bartoli's gallery. She was gratified to see Maceo's eyes open wide in surprise and saw him suppress a smile. He turned to the middle-aged man, who was eyeing Ori both suspiciously and appreciatively. Ori knew immediately that this would be easy.

In less than a half hour, the man went away that satisfied his painting was the original (It was. Ori, knew an original Kahlo when she saw it.) and Maceo was grinning broadly as he poured them some drinks in his office.

He handed her a flute of champagne. "Thank you, Ori"

"Anything to help *Lucia*," she said smoothly but with a grin, and he laughed. He indicated her suit.

"That works"

She rolled her eyes. "If you have a secretary fetish, keep it to yourself"

Maceo shrugged good-naturedly. "Fair enough. But seriously, thank you. Man, you'd think my reputation alone would be enough to convince these people that I don't trade in counterfeit goods, but there it is"

Ori considered. "Mr. Bartoli ... I'm just guessing. Some of these men who come back to your gallery angry and bitter ... would they happen to have attractive wives?"

Maceo's grin was wide and completely unrepentant, and Ori had to laugh. "Oh, you really are a man-whore. Glad to help, Maceo, but next time, keep your pecker in your pants"

She got up to leave, but Maceo put up his hands. "Wait, before you go ... Lucia tells me you've become fond of our city"

Ori sat down again. "I have. It's beautiful and restful and serene"

Maceo laughed. "Not during Carnevale"

Ori grinned. "That's what Lucia said. What's your point?"

Maceo sat back. Ori tried not to look at the open neck of his shirt or the swarthy skin of his chest. "I want to offer you a job, Ori. I need a curator to work ahead of our current schedule and line up exhibits months, even years, in the future. You have contacts at MOMA and the Guggenheim, right?"

Ori nodded, her interest piqued. "All of the big guns, plus a lot of the small galleries"

"Contacts like those are invaluable" Maceo sighed, his handsome face serious for once. "Ori, we put together the exhibition we have now by the skin of our teeth. We simply don't have the time to fill our schedule at the moment, which means we miss out on the best pieces. I need someone like you, not just for the big names but as a scout finding new talent, as well as negotiating with galleries worldwide"

Ori was speechless for a moment. Maceo Bartoli, whether he knew it or not, had just described her dream job. Actually, dream job didn't even *begin* to cover it. And this man, this charming, gorgeous, yet completely untrustworthy man, was offering it to her right here, right now.

She narrowed her eyes at him. "Forgive me for asking ... you know if I work for you that there's even less a chance of me sleeping with you, right?"

For a moment, she wished she could take back the words because maybe, just maybe, she saw a little hurt in his eyes. But a second later Maceo smiled, and the cocky businessman was back.

"So does that mean that until you start work for me, there *is* a chance?"

Ori couldn't help but chuckle at him. "Absolutely none. Can I think about the job?"

Maceo smiled. "Of course. May I at least take you to dinner to say thank you for tonight?"

God, it was tempting, but if she let him wine and dine her, there was no way she'd be able to resist that smile, that body, those green, green eyes ...

"I can't. But thank you"

He nodded. "Then let me call you a water taxi"

He kissed her hand before she got into the water taxi and, as she was driven away through the canals, she looked back toward the dock. He was still there, watching her. He raised his hand and, unthinkingly, Ori did the same. Before she even made it back to her apartment, she knew she would tell him yes to the job.

And not just because it was her dream job.

ORI NEVER SAW the man in the shadows outside the apartment. He watched her go in and lock the door after herself. Then, as lights came on in the first-floor window, he smiled to himself. He walked a little down the street so he could not be seen or heard if she came out onto the balcony. He hoped she would—the girl was a looker, all right.

He pulled his cell phone out. "It's me. Yeah. You can tell him it's confirmed. His stepdaughter is in Venice, as we thought. What does he want me to do?" He listened carefully and began to smile. "Yeah, okay. Twenty-four hours"

He shut off his phone and stared up at the balcony. "Come on, Juliet. Show Romeo something here"

He grinned as Ori, now changed into a slouchy sweater and pajama pants, stepped out onto the balcony, a cup of steaming tea in her hands. Her dark hair tumbled over her shoulders. The observer felt his groin tighten. No wonder Janek wanted her found.

He almost felt sorry for the girl. He was absolutely sure that Janek didn't have good things planned for this little beauty. Not good things at all.

ORI LEANED her hot forehead against the cool tiles of the shower. The water spray was hot against her skin, but she barely felt it, concentrated as she was on imagining Maceo Bartoli's hands where hers were now between her legs, relentlessly massaging her clit until her vision exploded with stars and she gasped through her orgasm. She panted for air, reveling in the sensation.

Goddamn you, Maceo Bartoli. Her dreams had been full of him—mostly a continuation from last night. Him stopping her before she left his office, reaching around and freeing her hair from its bun, tugging open the white blouse, tiny white buttons flying everywhere. Her pushing him into his chair and straddling him; his cock filling her ...

"Oh, goddamn you, Maceo Bartoli," she whispered as another orgasm ripped through her. She'd woken up hornier than she had been in years—maybe even ever. For a second now, as she panted her way back to sanity, she wondered whether she should just go ahead and fuck him. Tell him no strings, no need to call. Just a sensational, mind-blowing fuck.

She laughed out loud. "What is the matter with you, girl?" She dressed quickly in sweats and set out to clean the entire apartment, distracting herself. Mid-morning, she heard her phone beep and checked it.

Made up your mind yet?

She grinned. *About the job? Yes. I'll take it. Thank you.*

Good. See you Monday ... unless I can persuade you to join me for dinner tonight?

Yes, yes, yes. *Mr. Bartoli, I don't think that is a good idea.*

Take a risk ...

Ori felt her heart beating hard against her ribs. *Oh, I want to. You don't know how much I want to ...* but she knew enough about powerful, rich men like Maceo to know that once she gave in to him ...

I can't.

Another time.

She was both grateful and regretful that he didn't try to persuade her.

Later, after the apartment was clean and she was filthy, she took a long soak, reading her book, then went out to the market to buy fresh fish and vegetables for her supper. While she was cooking she called AJ and was happy to hear him sounding upbeat and positive.

SHE WENT TO BED EARLY, falling asleep just after ten p.m. It was quiet outside, and she could hear the lapping of the water on the sides of the canal. It lulled her to sleep, but at a quarter of eleven, she awoke with a start. Someone was in the apartment. She could hear them moving in the other room.

She slid out of bed, looking around for a weapon. She grabbed a vase from the dresser and stole to the side of the door, peeking out. She held her breath ... but the fear was almost overwhelming, the memories of years ago when her stepfather was creeping down the hall to her bedroom.

Never again.

She drew in a deep breath then and, with a banshee howl, darted for her intruder. He picked her up easily, her size no match for his, and threw her across the room. Adrenaline made her leap back to her feet and she ran at his midsection, hearing a muffled *oof* as her head connected with his belly.

"Fucking bitch ..."

His hands were around her throat then, squeezing, squeezing ... until nothing. She could breathe again, and his weight was being pulled off her by someone else, someone shouting— a familiar voice.

Maceo.

The two men struggled as Ori tried to catch her breath. Then, with a roar, Maceo threw the man out into the hallway, and her attacker took off, cursing. Maceo locked the door behind him and came to her, wrapping his arms around her, calming her.

Confused, scared, and discombobulated, Ori let him hold her until she had calmed enough to meet his gaze. Maceo opened his mouth to speak. Instead, Ori, driven by terror, lust, and chaos, pressed her lips to his hungrily. He took her face in his hands as he kissed her, and they only broke apart when they ran out of air.

Maceo, his green eyes full of desire but at the same time questioning, spoke softly. "Are you sure?"

Ori nodded, her body curving around his. In one easy motion, Maceo swept her into his arms and carried her to the bedroom. Ori didn't care that she was in her old ratty-but-comfortable T-shirt and shorts combo; all her attention was on the man above her. Maceo pulled his T-shirt off in one easy motion, and Ori saw the finely-honed planes of his body and his thickly muscled arms.

Maceo pushed her T-shirt up, pulling it over her head. And then his mouth was on her breasts, sucking each nipple, teasing them until she was moaning, his hands slipping inside the waistband of her shorts to stroke her clit. Oh god, it was even better than she had fantasized about, the rhythmic stroking of his long, strong fingers making her pussy soaking wet, her skin electrified by his touch.

Her hands fumbled at the zipper on his jeans. She could feel his cock hot and hard against the denim, and when she finally managed to make her trembling fingers free it from his underwear, she stroked the length of it, feeling it shudder and thicken under her touch.

"Ori ..."

His eyes were fixed on hers, the desire in them making her head swim. Ori stroked his face.

"Don't wait, Maceo, please ..."

He ripped her shorts from her and hitched her legs around his waist. Ori felt his cock nudge at her cunt then as he plunged into her. She gasped at the sensation of him filling her completely, of their bodies rocking in perfect symmetry, his lips against hers. Right this minute she didn't care about anything else but being fucked by this glorious, glorious man.

He drove himself into her, both of them delirious with desire, until they both came, crying out, his hands pinning hers to the bed. He barely let her recover before his tongue was lashing around her clit, driving her crazy.

Maceo Bartoli made Ori come four times before he finally let her catch her breath. Panting, she smiled up at him. "That was just a thank you, Mr. Bartoli, for, you know, saving my life"

He grinned down at her. "Well, then, thank you back"

They rested for a while, Maceo's arm around her, her head nestled on his shoulder. Then he moved away, propped himself up on his elbow, and looked down at her. "Ori ... who was that man?"

She shook her head, her smile fading. "I honestly don't know. I woke up and he was in the apartment. I attacked him first, so I could argue that he wasn't violent until I was" She sighed and sat up, rubbing her eyes, totally at ease with being naked with this man. She smiled at him and touched his cheek. "Thank you, Maceo, really ... but can I ask? Why were you here?"

Maceo looked sheepish. "Call me old-fashioned, but knowing you were here alone … it bothered me. So, I just took a late-night boat ride"

"I've been alone for a couple of days … did you do that last night too?"

He nodded, looking up at her from beneath his thick dark eyelashes in a way that made her belly quiver with desire. "Forgive me"

Ori wasn't sure how she felt about his vigilance, but she couldn't deny that tonight, it had saved her life. Maceo sat up now and kissed her shoulder. "I'm not sure this is the safest place for you," he murmured, his lips against her skin. His long fingers stroked her belly, making it vibrate with desire. "Why don't you come back to mine?"

She was tempted, sorely tempted, but she shook her head. "I don't think that's a good idea. I mean, I don't want to give the impression that I can't look after myself. Tomorrow, I'll go get a deadbolt"

Maceo sighed, running a hand through his dark curls. "Simpler to stay with me"

She looked around at him and smiled. "Maceo, on Monday morning you'll be my boss. I don't think it's advisable to be sleeping with the boss"

Maceo was silent, his lips still on her shoulder, his light green eyes fixed her hers. Goddamn, he really knew how to work that whole smoldering Italian thing …

"Fine," he said suddenly. "But I'm staying tonight"

Ori was strangely relieved. "Thank you. I'd like that"

He pulled her back down onto the bed, on top of him. "And also, I'll get my people to find out who your intruder was. If you like, we can go to the *polizia*. But I warn you, a case like this, they won't spend a lot of time on it. That's just the way things are here"

He was trailing his fingers up and down her spine, which was distracting Ori so much that she agreed without even listening and soon his mouth was on hers, and he was rolling her onto her back.

They made love long into the night and Maceo was both tender and rough, attending to every part of her body, challenging her to do things she had never dreamed of. Ori knew in her heart that she'd probably never have another night like this, with a man who awoke in her a primal need and a feral desire such as this. Maceo Bartoli deserved his legendary 'swordsman' status. His cock, huge and proud, plunged deep inside her relentlessly, making her crazy, and she gave herself up to him entirely for the rest of the night.

ORI'S ATTACKER, humbled and bleeding, knocked on the hotel suite's door. He'd ignored the curious stares of the staff at reception as he had limped towards the elevator; the night manager had approached him, but he had warned him off with a *don't-fuck-with-me* stare.

A bald, gigantic henchman opened the door of the suite, smirking when he saw the man's wounds.

"Got your ass handed to you by a girl, did you?"

"Shut the fuck up, moron. Is he here?"

"Ready and waiting"

The man walked into the suite's living room. Tyson Janek was impeccably dressed, even at this late hour, in a Saville Row suit, a heavy glass of bourbon n his hands. He stood with back facing the room, but turned as the man greeted him. His steel gray eyes were cold.

"Where is my stepdaughter?"

"She attacked me, and then her boyfriend got involved. I thought it best to back off and re-evaluate"

Janek's face was expressionless. "My stepdaughter does not have a boyfriend, Mr. Harrison. Are you telling me that there was a man with her tonight?"

Harrison nodded.

Janek put his glass down on the table. "Filthy little whore," he whispered, almost to himself. He was silent for a few long moments, then looked back at Harrison. "Find out who the boyfriend is and end him"

Harrison—who had no trouble killing women, but balked at taking on men twice his size—looked alarmed. "Sir, I think that might be a mistake"

Janek looked faintly amused. "You do?"

Harrison kept his mouth shut, knowing this look of old. It was the calm before the storm. Janek would appear amused, then from nowhere would explode into a rage which made Hurricane Katrina look like a brief rain shower.

Janek picked up his glass. "So, she has a boyfriend. I knew the blessed little virgin act wouldn't last" He considered, then glanced back at Harrison. "Fine. Keep watching them, but I want to know everything about the boyfriend"

Harrison was relieved. "Consider it done"

WHEN HE WAS ALONE, Janek brooded, nursing another drink. He had come to Italy after a mutual friend had told him he'd seen Ori in the city— *alone,* the friend had told him. Tyson Janek had seen his political career collapse because of his affairs with the wives of his friends, but he was convinced he could turn things around in a year or two. After all, who would honestly care about it after the initial scandal? How many times had JFK fucked up? And yet he was still considered a god.

Tyson went to his bathroom now and stripped off. At fifty-five, he was still hard-bodied and had the handsome, all-American good looks that had propelled his career so far. Even now, so near to the scandal, people were already whispering that he was so good-looking, who could blame those women for falling for him? Who could blame a red-blooded male for taking advantage of what was thrown in his path?

Once Kathryn had—fortuitously, in Tyson's opinion—died young of cancer, he had been able to focus all of his attention on Ori. On those nights he used to go to her room, force the door open, and see her cowering on her single bed, there was no one to hear him and stop him then. Nor would there be now ...

When she left home—practically the day she turned sixteen—Tyson had lost some of that control over her, but while AJ was still under his parentage, he knew he could still be sure that Ori would not tell anyone about Tyson's particular peccadillos.

Now AJ had left home and Tyson no longer had that assurance. Which was why, regrettably, his beautiful Orianthi would have to die.

He stepped into the shower, cranking the hot water on. As he stood under the spray, he imagined the leverage that a tragic death in the family would give him. All sins would be forgiven as the courageous, devastated congressman bravely vowed to find out who murdered his beautiful stepdaughter. And now that she had a boyfriend, he suddenly realized, he had someone to pin it on, to frame when they found Ori's broken, brutalized body.

Tyson grinned to himself as he shampooed his hair. *Perfect,* he thought. *Perfect.* Now he just had to pick the perfect time to kill her. Harrison was willing, if not eager to do it, but Janek had turned him down. "As much as I admire your bloodlust, Harrison, I will be the one to end Orianthi's life"

He couldn't wait.

WHEN ORI WOKE in the morning, the bed beside her was empty.

For a long moment, she fought with both disappointment and acceptance. *It's for the best,* she told herself. Maybe Maceo understood that this could not be a thing if they were to work with each other. She pushed the sheet back and swung her legs over the side of the bed just as she heard the door to the apartment open and his voice calling, "Good morning, beautiful"

Ori flushed, her heart leaping with joy. She padded barefoot into the living area to see him dumping fresh breakfast rolls onto a plate, a jug of orange juice already on her table. Maceo switched her coffee pot on and grinned at her. She laughed softly.

"Domesticated"

Maceo laughed. "No, just a hungry man. I need some energy after last night. Come here to me" He held out his arms but Ori backed off, grinning.

"Two seconds to brush my teeth, I have morning breath"

He held up his hands. "I don't care, but okay, go do what you have to"

Ori scooted into the bathroom and brushed her teeth, trying to get a handle on what she was feeling. *Thoroughly and professionally fucked, for one,* she grinned to herself now, as she rinsed her mouth. Her thighs ached and her vagina throbbed from the pounding Maceo's huge and ramrod hard cock had given it. Jeez ... even thinking about it made her wet again.

Her smile faded when she noticed the bruises on her neck and the clearly defined fingerprints. Jeez, what a whirlwind. *One minute I was being murdered, the next fucked to within an inch of my life.* Who the hell had broken into her apartment and why had he tried to kill her?

An image of her stepfather flashed into her mind. *No.* He had no idea where she was ... did he? Surely now that he was in disgrace, a lot of the contacts he could have used to find her had vanished—mostly because he'd fucked their wives. A wave of nausea hit her, and she gripped the side of the washbasin to steady herself.

"Are you okay, *bella*?"

Ori looked up to see Maceo watching her with concerned eyes. She smiled weakly at him. "I think the break-in just hit me"

He came to her then, his fingers brushing her bruised neck. "I won't let anything happen to you, Ori. I promise" God, she could get lost in his green eyes…

Maceo brushed his lips against hers. He tasted of fresh air. Ori closed her eyes and reveled in his kiss, his tongue gently massaging hers, his hands dropping to her waist and pulling her close to him. She could feel his erection through his clothes, hot and long against her belly. *What this man does to me …*

She gave a little moan, which seemed to spur him into action. Pulling her T-shirt over her head in one swift motion, he lifted her up so her buttocks rested on the sink. Ori kept her mouth on his as he eased her shorts off and tugged her legs around his waist. And then he was inside her again, impaling her on his long shaft. Ori cried out as he fucked her hard, his thickly muscled arms lifting her small frame easily, his mouth rough on hers.

He took her again in the shower they shared, pressing her against the cool tile as he thrust into her from behind, murmuring her name again and again until she was almost crying with pleasure.

They devoured the breakfast rolls hungrily afterward, and Maceo told her some more about her new job. "I think we will be working together very closely," he said with a wicked grin. "I need someone to travel the world with me, to go and scout the cities while I deal with the red tape and business side. It is regretful that I cannot make the time to see all the galleries—that is my first love—but it's not what made me a billionaire"

Ori was curious. "Do you come from a rich family?"

Maceo shook his head. "My mother looked after me on her own and gave me a good upbringing, but we did not lead a wealthy life. It made me determined to give her everything. I am glad I got to spoil her before she passed"

Ori felt a wash of sympathy. "I'm sorry she's gone, Maceo"

He nodded, comfortable with his emotions. "What about you?"

Ori shifted in her chair. "My mom died a few years ago. I have a younger brother— well, half-brother, AJ He's the love of my life, really" She was grinning now, thinking of him, and Maceo smiled at her.

"I can see that. Lucia tells me your stepfather is a politician"

Ori's smiled faded and unconsciously, she touched the bruises at her neck. "My mother is dead. He's no longer my stepfather"

Maceo covered her hand with his. "I understand, *bella*" He leaned over to kiss her. "Now, by your own logic, I'm not your boss until Monday morning, and it just so happens that I have the weekend free. Would you spend it with me, Ori? I would like to show you my *Venezia*"

Ori smiled at him, grateful for the change of subject. "Yes, Maceo, I would like that very much"

A LITTLE WHILE LATER, when Ori had excused herself to use the bathroom, Maceo pulled out his cell phone. In a low voice, he instructed his private detective to find out everything he could on Tyson Janek. "I want to know where he is, what he wants ... and what the hell he's been doing to his stepdaughter"

"MR. MILLAND, would you come this way?" The police captain came to greet him personally and led him to his office. After they had been seated, the captain gave him a sympathetic look.

"Mr. Milland, I know this has been hard, but I assure you that we are doing everything we can to find Viola's killer"

"It's been weeks and no new leads," Alex said. "Surely there must be something. Can you trace the crossbow bolt?"

"Unlikely," the captain said. "Mr. Milland, can you think of anyone or anything, no matter how seemingly inconsequential that might make—"

"Someone fire a crossbow bolt into the abdomen of the woman I loved? No," Alex was snippy now. "Viola had no enemies. None. And to do that to someone ... why?"

The police captain hesitated. "Mr. Milland, our police psychologist has been asking the same questions"

"And?"

"The manner of killing ... the way she was tied before being shot ... he seems to think it was a sexual motive"

Alex leaned forward. "Aren't they all? Viola was a beautiful woman, Captain. I assumed it was sexually motivated from the beginning. The question is—who?"

The captain tapped his pen on the desk. "Mr. Milland, how long had you and Viola been in a relationship?"

"Two years, five months, and seven days. Why?"

"Is it possible she had a lover? Or lovers?"

Alex felt the blood drain out of his face, but he sighed. "It's possible. I spent long days and nights away on business. We sometimes argued about it" He turned hooded, haunted eyes to the captain. "Am I a suspect?"

"We can't rule out anyone at this point"

Alex nodded. "I understand"

"Do you know of anyone close to you who might have had the opportunity—I'm not saying they did anything untoward—but had the opportunity to be alone with Viola?"

Alex rubbed his head. "Yes. I have a group of friends with whom Viola was friendly, and I know when they were in town and I wasn't, they would sometimes have dinner or drinks with her. But none of them would do this, Captain. They are my brothers"

"It would be good to talk to them, Mr. Milland"

Alex shook his head. "No, I won't believe any of them had anything to do with this. You're looking in the wrong direction"

"Still, Mr. Milland ... I'd like to have their names. Just to be thorough" The captain's voice had taken on a hard edge and Alex, seeing how seriously he was taking this, couldn't think of a way to dissuade him.

"Please don't harass them," he said and, sighing, began to recite their names. "Lisander Duarte, Benoit Vaux, Seth Cantor, Maceo Bartoli ..."

AFTER A WEEKEND of sightseeing and screwing—sometimes both at the same time— Ori finally sent Maceo home on Sunday evening. "I don't want anyone to know we've been together," she said firmly, "I need to make my own first impression. I don't want to be known as the girl who screwed her way into her job, Maceo"

Maceo had no choice but to honor her wishes, but he insisted on making sure the apartment was intruder-proof before he left. Ori didn't mind that at all. Seeing Maceo working with his hands, fixing deadbolts to the door, installing an alarm, especially when he could have just paid someone to do it, was a huge turn on. She thanked him profusely in the shower afterward.

Now, as she sat outside on the balcony breathing in the cool night air, she missed him. His crazy, infectious energy was like a balm to every bad thing. Yes, she knew that she was unlikely to ever be able to trust him completely ... but when had she trusted anyone, anyway? Even her beloved mother had let her down the one time Ori had gone to her and told her what Tyson had done to her.

"You must never, ever say anything like that ever again, child, never"

And, haunted by the fear on her mother's face, she hadn't.

Maceo Bartoli ... he had gotten under her skin in a way Ori had never experienced before. She was under no illusions that they were dating—they were merely screwing—no commitment, no relationship, and that was fine with her. But she couldn't stop thinking about the way his lips felt against hers, or the clean scent of his skin, and the way his gaze fixed on hers as he thrust into her. She could still feel the way his dark brown curls felt as she slid her fingers through them. *God, stop thinking about him,* she told herself fiercely—even dreaming of him turned her on.

She went to bed early, setting her alarm for seven a.m. She had a water taxi booked for eight; she wanted to be early on her first day. Her work clothes—a simple burgundy dress and heels—hung on the back of her door. Ori got into bed and switched off the lamp, scooching down. She felt optimistic for the first time in a long time. A new job, a new life. A new love? Her cell phone beeped with a text message.

Goodnight, sleeping beauty. I will see you in the morning. Sleep well, M.

Ori smiled to herself and replied. *You too ... boss*. She put a smiley face on the end of the message and shut off her phone. Soon she was asleep, the cool Venice air drifting in through the window.

She had no idea how soon her happiness would be shattered.

. . .

TYSON JANEK STOOD on the small boat as it pulled up alongside the jetty outside Ori's apartment, but he made no move to get out. Instead, he stared up at the open window of where she had to be sleeping. *So close ...*

So she'd scored herself a billionaire boyfriend, then? *Maceo Bartoli.* Tyson's murderous jealousy had not been helped by what Harrison had discovered about the man. He was 39, an art dealer and gallery owner, involved in something called The Midnight Club. Bartoli was powerful, had friends in the Italian government, and was a ruthless businessman. But all that was nothing compared to Bartoli's almost legendary status with women. If he wanted them, he could have them—his devastating good looks made sure that the world's most beautiful women hung on his every word.

And now he had Ori. *My Ori*, Tyson seethed, but he did not show it on his face. He wondered if Bartoli would be unhappy when Ori died or if she was just another random fuck for him.

No. From the personality profile he had on the man, Bartoli might be a whore, but he treated all his castoffs royally. He was passionate and caring, even if commitment wasn't his thing. Tyson had to admit, he probably suited Ori. Ori had always hated being tied down—Tyson smirked to himself, *and literally too.*

He nodded to the boat captain, who backed the small boat away from the jetty and out into the lagoon. No, Maceo Bartoli would mourn Ori, Tyson was sure.

But he'll mourn her from the confines of a jail cell.

ORI WALKED into the gallery at a quarter of nine, nervous but excited. She saw Maceo already there, talking to a group of people gathered around one of the paintings. Clients, she guessed, and hovered in the background, not sure of what to do.

She watched Maceo charm them, making them laugh, the women all tucking their hair behind their ears and standing a little straighter. Ori hid a smile. *Man whore in everything,* she thought without malice. She could see the danger of him—so easy to fall for, so difficult to let go.

Maceo noticed her, and a huge smile spread across his face. He excused himself politely and came to her. "And early, too. That's always a plus" He kissed her cheeks, his green eyes twinkling at her. "Come meet some people and then we'll get to organizing you"

The morning flew by as Ori didn't have the time to worry as Maceo steered her through meeting clients and getting to know the staff. He introduced her as a friend of Lucia's; she was glad, it saved her a lot of nervousness. Maceo, his hand on the small of her back, was professional all the way, and most of the young woman greeted her as an old friend. Ori wasn't stupid; she knew Maceo had probably screwed half, if not more, of them, but to his credit, they all seemed to be on friendly terms with their boss. Only one woman, Cassie—the other American—Maceo had chuckled – a blonde with a sweet face, was cooler to Ori, her eyes searching her face, then resting on Maceo. A small smirk hitched up at the side of her mouth. Ori flushed, but Maceo didn't notice anything.

"Cas, can I get you to show Ori somewhere she can dump her things? She'll be hot-desking mostly for now. Ori, please excuse me for a few more moments while I show my clients out"

"Of course"

Cassie took Ori up a flight of glass stairs. A large open plan office lay on the second floor but Ori was amused to see huge tables filled with art materials as well as the usual desks. It was messy and colorful and Ori loved it. A few of the women working up there looked at her curiously. Cassie showed her a desk in the corner, a view out to the lagoon a welcome sight to the cramped space.

"You can use this one," Cassie told her. "Maceo doesn't care how you personalize it as long as you're happy—but it doesn't sound like you'll be using it a lot. I hear you're to be our new scout?"

Ori detected an undertone to her words but decided to ignore it. She didn't want to fall out with anyone on her first day. "Apparently so. I'm excited to start"

Cassie took her through the computer and phone system, then showed her the bathrooms and kitchen, making them both a rather weak coffee. Ori sipped it, grateful despite the taste. Her nerves had only gotten worse since she got to the gallery. Cassie left her alone at her desk, and Ori took the chance to catch her breath and survey her surroundings. A small dark girl waved at her from across the room, and Ori smiled at her. The girl came over and sat on Ori's desk.

"Hello, I'm Sirena, Maceo's intern. Anything you need, just ask. I love your scarf"

Ori smiled at her. Sirena had a warm, friendly face, and merry, twinkling eyes. "I will, thank you"

They chatted easily for a few minutes before Maceo reappeared and spirited Ori away to his office. She was glad to see that the door had no window in it because as soon as it was shut, Maceo pushed her up against it and kissed her. She responded to his lips, but then gently pushed him away. "Maceo ... I don't think this appropriate at work"

Mace grinned good-naturedly and steered her to the couch. "Fair enough ... although, seeing you in that dress, damn ..." He leaned across to nuzzle her neck, and she couldn't resist the feel of his lips on her throat. "I want to be inside you, Ori ...'"

Her moan of desire gave her away, and in one movement she was under him. Mace pushed the skirt of her dress up as she fumbled with his fly and in seconds, he was thrusting into her. It was a quick, hard, dirty fuck, which left them both laughing and panting for air.

As she tidied herself up afterward, feeling his cum start to trail down her thigh, she rammed her legs together and gave him a disapproving look. "You just broke all my rules"

Maceo was grinning and unrepentant. "*Bella*, you have this effect on me. I cannot help how I feel. Now." He sat down behind his desk and pulled her down onto his lap, "Tomorrow you and I fly to Paris. I have meetings set up for us all day at the George V. Potential new clients, all of them. Then the next day, we will scout some Parisian artists. My friend Benoit is already looking forward to seeing you again"

Maceo, Ori was discovering, worked at breakneck speed. "Paris? Tomorrow?"

Maceo grinned. "I told you this would be an exciting opportunity. We fly at ten a.m."

ORI STEPPED out onto the balcony of their hotel suite. Paris, its lights twinkling in the dusk, stretched out before her. She breathed in the cool night air and listened to the sounds of the traffic drifting up from the streets below. They had been here for two days, and it had been a dream. Meeting prospective clients had been nerve-racking, but she found Maceo could charm anyone. He was aware of her nerves and guided her through the meetings, giving her tips on what the clients liked and what they expected, and soon she was finding her footing. They had dinner with a couple of Maceo's oldest and most loyal customers, and then Maceo had taken her back to their suite and fucked her brains out all night long.

Ori laughed to herself now. She couldn't describe it any other way. Maceo, his grin broad and confident, had taken her on the floor, against the wall, in the shower— even, when the night was darkest, out here on the balcony, muffling her cries of pleasure with his hand so they didn't draw attention to themselves. She shivered now, reliving the pleasure of his cock driving into her, his strong hands on her body.

She started as he slid his arms around her waist now, kissing her ear, her neck, her shoulder.

"*Mio caro,*" he whispered, his fingers splaying out on her belly, warming her skin through her thin cotton dress. "Don't turn around"

Ori felt him ease her legs apart and lift her skirt from behind. She gazed out at the night as he slid gently into her and then she sighed as he began to move, one hand cupping her throat, his lips on her neck, the other hand finding her clit and kneading and rubbing until she was shuddering. She knew instinctively that this was not the time for screaming, but a slow, sensually journey to ecstasy.

She shivered through one, two, three orgasms as he murmured what he'd like to do to her, and she felt him stiffen before hot semen pumped deep into her belly. She leaned back into his big strong frame, breathing hard. Maceo kissed her cheek. "Are you okay?"

Ori laughed. "God, Maceo, how can you even ask? You're amazing"

"As are you, *mio caro*. Come, let's sit a while; we still have time before we have to change for dinner"

They were going out to eat with Maceo's friend Benoit and a date, and Ori was nervous and excited to finally see another part of Maceo's life.

Maceo lit a cigarette and gazed at her. "*Caro* ... would you do something for me?"

"Of course"

He leaned forward. "Would you strip for me?"

Ori was taken aback but smiled. "If you'd like"

She stood and slowly peeled her dress off, followed by her bra and panties, and stood before him. Maceo ran his eyes slowly over her body. "You are perfect. Do you know that?"

Ori laughed, embarrassed at the compliment but not about her nakedness. She could not feel shy with this man; he made her feel like a goddess. "Your eyesight may be failing you, old man," she joked, and Maceo grinned.

"If anything, it's improved. Come here to me" He held his arms out, and she slid onto his lap, curling up in his arms, totally vulnerable. "How is it no one has snapped you up, taken you to their castle, and hidden you away?"

Ori felt a jolt. An image of her stepfather flashed across her vision, binding her, holding her down, imprisoning her, and she suddenly felt exposed and ridiculous. She extracted herself from Maceo's arms and slipped her dress back on.

"*Caro,* did I say something to upset you?" His eyes were curious and concerned. She shook her head.

"It's not you, Maceo." She tried to smile at him, but he leaned forward.

"What is it?"

She shook her head. "Please, Maceo, let's not spoil our evening by talking about ... my past."

Another long pause. "As you wish."

AFTER THEY HAD CHANGED for dinner, mostly in thoughtful silence, Maceo took her hand. "I hope you will get to know Benoit better," he said. "He is one of my oldest friends."

Ori asked him about his and Ben's friendship.

"We met in college—he and I, and our other friends, Lisander, Seth, and Alex. All five of us were driven and knew what we wanted. And by and large, twenty-odd years later, we all have it. The press calls us The Midnight Club because we all share a birthday—same time of day as well as date and year."

Ori's eyes opened wide. "That's an incredible coincidence."

"Isn't it? We were obviously meant to be friends. When is your birthday, *mio caro*?"

"November 13th."

"I shall remember. Start thinking about where you would like to go."

Ori stopped him. "Maceo ... I know how the game is played. You don't have to say such things. I'm not looking for a commitment here ... and I know you're not."

There was an expression she couldn't read in his eyes. "I'm not?"

She kissed him. "It's okay, Maceo. It really is. I'm not naïve to the world, especially the world of a drop-dead gorgeous, *extremely* eligible billionaire like you. Why would you commit when you could have anyone? All I ask is that you're honest with me."

The elevator door opened as she finished speaking and Maceo, all humor gone from his face, was silent as they walked to their waiting cab. In the car on the way to the restaurant they didn't speak, but Maceo held her hand, his fingers knotted between hers. Ori glanced over at him as he stared out of the window. Maybe he'd never had a woman say that to him, and that's what was throwing him. Ori knew she had made the right decision to say what she had; it was a way of protecting her heart because, God knew, Maceo had been battering down the walls that she'd spent years building around it. She could not risk falling in love with him. She *would* not risk that.

At the restaurant, Benoit and his date were already waiting, and Maceo, his mood seeming to lighten, introduced her. Ori was touched by the note of pride she heard in his voice as he introduced her.

Benoit Vaux was in the same league as Maceo, she decided—charming, ruthless and devastatingly handsome. The two men shared the same brooding quality, but Benoit seemed more serious than Maceo. His date, Marcella, was an Audrey Hepburn lookalike, all grace and elegance, but a very sweet nature. Ori chatted happily with her as the two men talked about business.

"You have certainly made an impression on Maceo." Marcella told her, smiling, "I can't remember the last time he introduced us to a date."

Ori was surprised but kept her counsel. "How long have you and Benoit been together?"

Marcella smiled. "Oh, we're not together in that sense. I mean, we do spend time together, shall we say, but we're not a couple. Just very good friends. Benoit does not have the time to commit to a full relationship."

Ori frowned. "Like Maceo."

Marcella looked taken aback. "No, I don't think so. Anyway, my dear, to answer your question, Benoit pays very well for my company. Not that I wouldn't do it for free, you understand, but he insists."

An *escort?* This glamourous, elegant, intelligent woman?

Marcella chuckled. "The expression on your face is why I love to tell Americans the truth about Benoit and me, about what I do. He's quite open about it, you see? We're consenting adults."

Ori grinned. "Hey, no judgment here. As long as it's consensual, have at it."

"Being an escort is my choice, Ori, but it is not my occupation. I do it because I enjoy sex with handsome men. At the same time, I prefer to live alone."

They chatted a little while longer, then Ori remembered something. "Do you know anything about someone called Viola? I believe she was one of Maceo's friends?"

The smile faded from Marcella's face, and she sighed. "Poor girl. She was murdered—horribly, too—shot with a crossbow."

Ori felt sick. "God, who would do that?"

"They haven't found anyone responsible yet..." Benoit broke into their conversation, and Ori realized the two men had been listening to them. "Alex is a mess; until he knows why, he can't move past it."

The rest of the dinner was a more somber affair after that and Ori regretted asking. As she and Maceo were being driven back to the George V, she looked over at him. "Maceo?"

He smiled at her. "What is it, *bella*?"

"I'm sorry for asking about Alex's girlfriend."

"It's okay. It's playing on all of our minds."

"Did you know her well?"

He nodded, but said nothing more. He took her hand and kissed the back of her fingers. "*Caro*, there's something we need to talk about when we get to the hotel."

Ori's heart started to pound uncomfortably. *No, not yet. I'm not ready for you to dump me. Not here, not now, please ...* but she just smiled and said, "Okay."

IN THE HOTEL ROOM, he led her out to the balcony and pulled her onto his lap. "Ori, something has been bothering me this evening. I hope I didn't ruin our evening."

"Of course not, Maceo, but what's wrong?"

Maceo sighed. "I know how people see me, and a lot of it has to do with my past behavior. With the opposite sex, I mean. I'm sure Lucia warned you away from me."

Ori grinned, hoping to lighten the atmosphere by teasing him. "*Warned* doesn't really cover it."

Maceo gave a small chuckle. "You see? What chance do I stand? But, Ori, these last few days with you ... I feel so differently that I'm having trouble reconciling it. You make me want to see if I could do it, if I could commit."

Ori stared at him, shocked. "What?"

He rolled his eyes. "I'm telling you I'm crazy about you, Orianthi Roy."

Every emotion that flooded her body left her speechless. *No. No, this was a line ... surely? This was what men like him did—made you fall for them and then dumped you. It was a game. Maceo was a world-class player.*

"I don't believe you," she said flatly and slid from his arms, pacing the room.

Maceo watched her, his eyes never leaving her face. "Why is so hard to believe that someone might love you, Ori?"

She didn't answer him, just turned hurt eyes on him. "Don't. Please, Maceo...."

"It's your stepfather, isn't it?"

Ori felt all the air being pushed out of her lungs. Maceo saw through her to the frightened little girl that she was. She stared at him but saw no malice in his looks. He stood and came to her, but she backed away. *Don't touch me or I'll break.*

Her back hit the wall, but Maceo wouldn't let her run, trapping her in the cage of his arms. "*Bella. Mio amata ...*" His voice was soft and tender. "What the hell did he do to you?"

Ori stared back at him, her eyes filling with tears. "Maceo ... please don't do this. I can't."

He stroked her face. "I can see it in your eyes, my love. Whatever that man has done to you, I'll make him pay for it."

She pushed her way out of his arms. "Don't promise things you can't deliver."

Maceo sighed. "Why are you so afraid of sharing your life with me?"

"I'm not ready!" she exclaimed, pain shooting through her. "If I tell you, it'll make it real and...." Tears came now, and she choked on her words. Her cell phone beeped and, grateful for the distraction, she picked up the phone. Voicemail. She listened to it, her face pale.

Maceo watched the different emotions running across her face and waited until she ended the call. "It's AJ," she said in a dull voice, "He's in a rehab facility in New York. That was his physician. He's had a relapse in his depression. He needs me. Maceo, I'm sorry. I have to go to him."

Maceo nodded. "Of course, we will fly out immediately."

We? Ori closed her eyes. "No, Maceo, I can't let you get involved. It's too much to ask."

But Maceo would not be shut out and a couple of hours later, they were on a plane to the States.

Ori was in turmoil. On the one hand, she was grateful to Maceo for his kindness. On the other, she didn't want to drag him into this part of her life, the part where she was unhappy, into her family drama. If Tyson knew about Maceo, who knew what he would do? Tyson Janek was violently jealous and possessive over Ori. He had paid past boyfriends off, or blackmailed them into leaving her alone. She knew Maceo would not be so easily gotten rid of, and it frightened her to think what depths Tyson would sink to. The thought of anything happening to Maceo ... Ori knew then, at that moment, that the worst thing had happened. She was in love with Maceo Bartoli.

She closed her eyes, willing the tears not to come, but then felt his lips on her forehead. "Tell me," he said softly, and wrapped his arms around her. And so, in the confines of his private jet, Ori told him the horrors of her family, of how broken she was, and how her stepfather had tormented her, her whole life.

"WHAT DO you mean he's not here?" Ori's voice was growing

shriller by the minute as she stood in the very well-appointed reception of the Pinegap Rehabilitation Facility. The director looked at her with sympathy.

"I'm sorry, Ms. Roy. Mr. Janek removed his son from the facility yesterday; as he has power of attorney, there was nothing we could do. I do have some of Adam's possessions that he forgot in a rush. Would you like to take them to him?"

Ori nodded, feeling bleak. Tyson had done this on purpose, to show her he was still in control. She guessed he would not easily give up where AJ was. Maceo stood beside her silently, his hand on the small of her back protectively. She looked at him and shook her head, and he nodded. She wanted to scream and rant, but she was damned if she would do it here.

The director came back with a plastic bag. "Just a few items, but he may want them in the future."

Ori thanked the director, and she and Maceo returned to Maceo's town car. Ori opened the bag and took out an empty money clip, a copy of *The Sun Also Rises* (AJ's favorite book), and the burner phone she had gotten him.

"Fuck that bastard," she hissed and showed Maceo the phone. "He knew AJ and I would talk. He's cutting us off from each other."

Maceo looked angry. "Bella, I will help you find him. I have a fleet of private investigators here in New York that I can put on the case right now, if you'd like. Janek won't be able to hide AJ forever."

Ori smiled at him gratefully. "That would be wonderful, Maceo. I can't thank you enough; I'm sorry you had to get involved in this bullshit."

"Don't be sorry; just be ready to fight." Maceo nodded grimly. "Because one way or another, Janek is going down."

. . .

AJ Janek sat on the bunk of his new cell. It was luxurious, he had to give his dad that, but cold and sterile. The reason he had chosen Pinegap was because it had outside space and places he could spend time sketching or watching the birds in the trees. Tyson had arrived yesterday and had barely given AJ the time to acknowledge his presence before he was whisked away in Tyson's bulletproof car to this place. *Jesus ...*

AJ put his head in his hands. He didn't even have his phone to call Ori now. Tyson had forbidden calls, and the staff here was obviously under strict instructions not to help AJ at all. AJ wondered if this was even a hospital or just one of Janek's 'businesses' that he used to launder cash.

Yeah, Dad. I know all about the illegal activities. And you know that too, don't you? It's why you destroyed my peace of mind and undermined my confidence so much so I couldn't function. And what you did to me and Ori? What would the good people of the United States think of the congressman if they knew the real truth?

Despair flooded through him, and he slumped back on his bed. *What the hell am I going to do now?* He hoped that when Ori discovered he was gone from Pinegap that she would come for him, but he knew without a doubt that Tyson would try to stop her—and AJ was under no illusions of the grotesque ways in which his father would try to stop her.

Ori had insisted on going to see Tyson, demanding to know where her brother was. "I don't want him to even think for a moment he has won," she raged to Maceo. "I'm going to go in there, to his office, in front of his staff, and demand he tells me."

Maceo wasn't enamored of the idea, but knew he wouldn't be able to stop her. "At least let me come with you."

Ori shook her head. "No, not this time, Maceo. Don't get me wrong. I'm so grateful that you're helping me, but I want to keep you as my secret weapon. So far, no one knows we are together. Tyson will threaten me and tell me I'm powerless, that I have no one. I want to see his face when I drop you on him."

Maceo nodded slowly. "Okay, I can get on board with that. Just ... I worry about your safety."

"Which is why I'll make sure I confront him in front of people." She kissed Maceo gently. "I will be fine."

"Take a recording device, or keep your phone on. Record every word he says. It might turn out to be useful."

So, when Ori walked into Tyson Janek's office the next day, she was wearing a wire. Downstairs, Maceo and one of his private detectives sat in his car, listening. Ori marched straight to Maceo's secretary, a thin-lipped blonde who had never liked her.

"Janine, please tell my stepfather I would like to see him."

"Do you have an appointment?" Janine shot back spitefully. Ori gave her a wintry smile and fixed her with a stare.

"*Now*, Janine." Ori's voice was low but full of threat and Janine sighed, pushing back her chair and getting up.

"Wait here, please."

Oh, I will. Ori gritted her teeth. Janine disappeared into Janek's office for a moment and Ori could hear her nasal whine through the open door.

"Orianthi, come in, please."

Oh, no. "I'd like to speak to you out here, Congressman."

"I'm very busy, Orianthi. Please come in and stop wasting time."

Fuck. Sighing, Ori pushed past a smirking Janine, who closed the door behind her. Ori was alone with Tyson. He didn't look up for a second, scrawling on a pad in front of him. "Sit down, Ori."

She stayed standing, and when he finally looked up, he smirked. "Still playing childish games, I see."

"Where's AJ?" Ori was clenching her fists into balls, trying not to lose her temper. Tyson leaned back in his chair.

"He's safe. In a much better place than that two-bit facility he chose. Or did you choose it for him?"

Ori gritted her teeth. "He's an adult, Tyson. A legal adult. And even if he weren't...."

"... Even if he weren't, he would still be my son, Orianthi. *My* son, *my* blood. Do you think you have rights over my son?"

"He's my brother."

"Half-brother."

"Go fuck yourself, Tyson. I'll find him on my own."

Tyson laughed. "Such a potty mouth on such a pretty girl. And my, you do look ravishing ... perhaps you have been away? Italy, perhaps?"

Ori stopped. "What?"

Tyson's smiled dropped, and he suddenly stood and darted toward her. He gripped her hands and yanked her toward him. Ori gave a small cry of alarm. Tyson smiled.

"I know where you've been, Orianthi. I know who you've been fucking." He buried his face in her neck and breathed deeply. "You stink of your Italian billionaire; do you know that? Where was your concern for my son when you were spreading your legs for Maceo Bartoli?"

Tyson slipped his hand between her legs, grabbing at her crotch. His other hand snaked around her waist tightly. Ori struggled to free herself.

"Get off me, you bastard."

Tyson laughed, running his hands up and down her body. "This was mine well before he touched it," he growled. "It belongs to me." He stopped suddenly and ripped open her blouse. The wire she was wearing was pinned to her bra. Snarling, he grabbed it and yanked it free. Ori felt pure terror.

Tyson grabbed his letter opener and held it to her skin. "Fucking little bitch. Think you can win against me? Let me tell you something, little girl. I can end you whenever I want, and they wouldn't even find your body. No one would care. What would happen if I drove this into you right now? Would your bastard Italian come for me? Let him try."

Ori rammed her knee hard into Tyson's groin, and he buckled. Furious instead of scared now, Ori pulled her blouse together, fingers fumbling at the buttons. "That's the last time you will ever touch me," she said, her voice shaking. "Now, where is my brother?"

She knew Maceo had heard Tyson attack her, along with her wire being destroyed, and was on his way even now. It gave her strength she never knew she had. Tyson was recovering now, and he gazed at her with absolute malevolence. "I'll tell you, Ori. I'll tell you at the exact same time my knife sinks into your gut, you little bitch. When your blood is on my hands, that's when you'll know you will never be able to escape me. You'll never see AJ again."

At that moment the door burst open and Maceo, all terrible beauty and rage, flew into the room and knocked Tyson Janek across the room. Ori grabbed Maceo before he could launch another attack on her stepfather. "Maceo, stop. I'm okay. Let's go. This pathetic piece of shit isn't worth it; we'll find AJ on our own."

Maceo looked like he would like to pound Tyson into the ground but instead, he let Ori lead him out of the office. It was only when they reached the car that Ori started to tremble, as all the adrenaline left her body. As they drove back to the hotel, Ori told him everything.

"He threatened to kill you?" Maceo was beyond livid.

Ori gave a humorless laugh. "Not for the first time, Maceo. He's been doing that since he first raped me."

Maceo launched into a torrent of Italian curse words, some of which Ori understood, but mostly she just let him rant. Finally, he looked at her. "I want to kill him."

She touched his cheek. "You and me both, baby, but it won't help AJ. He's the priority."

THEY STAYED in New York for a week before finally catching a break. A woman, a secretary from Tyson's office, called Ori from a payphone. "I know what that bastard is like," she told Ori, "so please don't let him know I told you this." She told them where AJ was being 'held,' as she described it. "It's not even a real place, just one of your stepfather's tax wrangles."

Ori and Maceo traveled up to the place near Westchester with an entourage of Maceo's staff. They outnumbered Tyson's weak security team easily and then Ori was inside. She found AJ's cell, appalled that he was locked in. The half-siblings hugged each other. Ori saw how much weight AJ had lost, and despaired. Her brother looked close to the edge

"Come on. We're taking you out of here."

Maceo had arranged for them all to go to his friend Alex Milland's place for a time before deciding what to do next. "It will be safer for both of you," he said to Ori and AJ, who smiled at him.

"I like him," AJ said with a grin and Ori flushed with pleasure. Maceo immediately fell into the role of big brother with AJ and Ori couldn't help but be overwhelmed with gratitude.

ONE AFTERNOON, Ori was taking a nap. Maceo watched her sleep for a while, studying every curve of her face, every line, and the way her dark, thick lashes fell onto her cheeks. In his 39 years, he had never felt like this about anyone. It was overwhelming. He pressed his lips to her forehead, then went to find AJ

He found him in Alex's study, hunkered down with a pile of books on the table next to him. AJ grinned at him. "I hope Alex doesn't mind."

"He wouldn't. I'd hoped he'd be around more, but he's so tied up in the investigation to find Viola's killer."

AJ nodded, his smile fading. "Poor guy. Is that what the police came to see you about yesterday?"

"Yeah, they wanted to interview everyone Viola was friends or acquaintances with. I knew her first, you see, before Alex."

AJ looked at him with interest. "I saw a photograph of her; she looks like my sister."

Maceo nodded. "The resemblance is uncanny, actually, not just physically but personality-wise."

AJ looked bleak. "Maceo, Ori told me that my father threatened to kill her. I don't doubt for a second that he's capable."

"Nothing is going to happen to Ori, AJ. oI promise you that."

AJ stared out of the window. "I keep thinking ... I'm Ori's only tie to Dad. If it weren't for me, she could be free."

Maceo felt a jolt. "Kiddo, don't think like that. Ori would take your dad's abuse again and again as long as she had you."

There was a long silence. "He raped her."

"Yes."

"Do you think she was protecting me by not telling anyone? The police?"

Maceo felt awkward. "I don't know."

Another long silence. "Dad used to get in these rages after Ori left home. He would rant and rave and drink himself into oblivion while completely obsessing about her."

Maceo got the feeling that AJ was trying to tell him something. "AJ, whatever you need to get off your chest, if you need it to stay between you and me, that's okay."

AJ nodded, and in a halting voice he began to tell Maceo just how much of a monster Tyson Janek was.

"You're quiet," Ori said as they got into bed that night. "Is everything okay?"

Maceo tried to smile. "As long as you're with me, it is."

He smoothed his hand down her side, feeling the dip of her waist and the curve of her hips. "Orianthi Roy, it's been less than a month and look what you've done to me."

Ori smiled and pressed her lips to his. "Look what you've done *for* me. Thank you, Maceo. You've gone above and beyond for a girl you didn't know a few weeks ago."

"That's not possible," he joked, but then gathered her to him. "Ms. Roy, you have changed my life."

"And you mine," she smiled, as he rolled her onto her back, and wrapped her legs around him. Her body trembled at every silky touch of his hands and when his mouth found her nipples, she sighed and closed her eyes. *God, this man.* She gasped as his teeth grazed her nipples, one after another, then felt the thick, hot length of his cock against her thigh. How on earth could any woman let this man out of her life?

Maceo kissed her belly then moved down so he could take her clit into his mouth. She tangled her fingers in his hair as his tongue flicked around her clit, then plunged deep inside her, tasting her, making her crazy. She barely had to recover as Maceo moved up her body and pulled her legs tight around his waist. His cock, huge and throbbing, slammed into her, and she moaned as Maceo rammed his hips against hers, every nerve ending in her body on fire.

"Oh, god, *Maceo*...." She arched her back as she came, her belly against his, her vaginal muscles contracting around his cock, a hot rush overwhelming her, then the feeling of his seed spilling into her as Maceo groaned her name. She never wanted this moment to end, this perfect moment with this wonderful man.

They fell asleep in each other's arms soon afterward but, plagued by vicious nightmares, Ori slept badly and gave up at three a.m... Sliding carefully out of bed, she slipped into her T-shirt and shorts and wrapped her robe around her.

She padded down to the kitchen and opened the refrigerator for some milk. Pouring herself a glass, she set it down on the counter to put the milk carton away, not seeing the man sitting in the corner of the room.

"Hi, Ori."

She started with a small cry then, when she saw it was Alex Milland, she laughed a little. Hand on her chest, she smiled at him. "I didn't see you there. Sorry, I was just...." She indicated the glass, and he nodded.

"Sorry, I didn't mean to startle you. It's just for a moment, you looked just like her."

Viola. Ori's heart twisted in sympathy, and she went to sit by him at the long kitchen table. "Are you okay? We were hoping to see you for dinner."

Alex, his eyes tired and sad, tried to smile. "More wasted time, I'm afraid. Did Maceo talk to the police?"

"He did."

"Did you know he was the one who introduced me to Viola?"

Ori nodded. "I did."

"I was thinking about that just then when you came in and it made me wonder. Your resemblance to her...."

Ori suddenly saw where this was going and felt alarmed.

"Alex, you don't think Maceo could have had anything to do with her murder, do you?"

Alex sighed and rubbed his eyes. "No, of course not. It wasn't like that—more like, you're obviously his type, so then why did he give Viola up to me?."

Ori tried to smile. "We aren't the same person no matter how much we look alike, Alex."

"No, of course not. I'm sorry. I'm so tired that nothing makes sense anymore. Let's change the subject ... how's your brother?"

"Doing better," Ori smiled at him. "I think he's in love with your library."

Alex laughed. "Then he has good taste. You're always welcome to stay as long as you like."

"You're very kind. I really am sorry about Viola."

"Thank you." Alex drained his glass of scotch and stood. "I'm going to try and grab some sleep. See you in the morning."

"Good night."

Alone, Ori wandered into the living room and slipped through the French windows into the garden. The grounds were beautiful, but now, here in the moonlight, Ori felt as if she were being watched. Was it just paranoia? She had kept the shock of Tyson's threats internalized for the most part, not wanting to goad Maceo into doing something that would get him into trouble. But she was under no illusions that her stepfather meant her no harm. She could go to the press; her relationship with Maceo giving her some kind of credence, she supposed. The feminist in her cringed at that, but it was true. Maceo was as powerful as Tyson, if not more. His backing would mean they could take down Tyson—but there was still AJ to think about. He was Tyson's son, and Ori would hate to see him hounded by the press.

Sighing, she went inside and went to bed, snuggling into the warmth of Maceo's arms. Tonight was not the night to try and figure it all out. She was asleep long before Alex Milland opened the door to their room and looked in on them.

"I WANT TO FIND ANOTHER FACILITY," AJ told them over breakfast. "Somewhere that's hardcore, that Dad can't finagle his way into. I truly believe I can get past all this crap if I get the right help."

Ori put her hand over her brother's. "Whatever you want, AJ. I'm here for you."

"*We're* here for you," Maceo corrected with a grin. "You deserve the best, brother, and both of you ... you're not to worry about the cost. I have it covered. Just pick the best one for you, AJ, and we'll get you in there as soon as you want."

Ori, too emotional to speak, hugged Maceo and he kissed the top of her head. AJ looked at him admiringly. "Maceo, man, I don't know how to thank you."

A look passed between the two men of understanding, of brotherhood. Ori was aware they had talked, but she didn't want to intrude. She looked up at Maceo as AJ started to talk to Alex, and she pressed her lips to his. "I love you," she said quietly, and Maceo chuckled, his eyes shining.

"*Ti amo*," he murmured against her lips, and her heart soared. Maybe everything would be okay, after all.

A WEEK LATER—GOD, had it really only been three weeks since they met?—they were on their way back to Italy. AJ had been transferred to a facility in California and although Ori was reluctant to leave him, AJ had insisted she go back to her new life, her new job.

"Try not to dwell on Dad," he said. "He can't touch either of us now. Maceo is a good man. Enjoy yourself, Ori. You deserve every happiness."

Sometimes AJ seemed much wiser than his eighteen years, Ori pondered now as she sat beside Maceo on his private jet. Now her thoughts were turning back to her new job—and her old friend. Lucia had returned from Monte Carlo and had been amazed at Ori's news. Ori omitted the part where she and Maceo were sleeping together—*and in love,* Ori grinned to herself now. She wanted to tell Lucia that particular news face to face. She wondered if Lucia would be happy for her, or whether her friend would remonstrate with her for falling for her boss after Lucia's warnings.

She looked over at Maceo now. He looked glorious—but tired. He hadn't been sleeping well, she knew, and deep inside, she was worried because it seemed like it had been since the *I love yous* that he'd been restless. Was he regretting showing his hand so soon? He had said he was ready for commitment, but maybe it had all been too much. Her stepfather, AJ, the thing about Viola ... it was a lot to put on a man who only a few weeks ago had been carefree and screwing his way around the world's most beautiful women.

Ouch. Ori pushed that thought away. *No. Don't dwell. Just live and love and everything will be okay.*

Maceo looked up and caught her watching him. He grinned, and her insides went to mush. "Are you all right, *bella*?"

"I'm with you. Of course I'm okay."

Maceo put his laptop down and slid next to her, taking her in his arms. "*Il mio amore*, when we get back to Venice, I would like you to move in with me. I want to know you are safe every minute. I want you to *feel* safe. And loved. Above all else, loved."

Ori was floored and suddenly nervous. "Really?"

"Really."

As she looked into his sea-green eyes and at their honesty, she knew what her answer would be.

. . .

Lucia rolled her eyes but hugged Ori anyway. "I might have known. For what it's worth, I've never seen him like this before, so I guess it must be love."

Ori was relieved that her friend was okay with her sleeping with her boss. She and Maceo kept things professional at the office, and she was grateful that she was learning from him too. She saw the way he dealt with his clients. He was definitely on the side of the artists and got them the best deals while maintaining good relationships with his buyers. His team, too, was ultra-efficient, and Ori found them all inclusive and helpful. Even Cassie had seemed to change her mind about Ori, and now she enjoyed the other woman's company. They would often go for lunch together and talk about back home. Cassie was from Virginia, a Rhodes Scholar and art historian by education.

"I just wanted to come to Italy to travel, but then I met Maceo and that was that."

"Snap,." said Ori, smiling, but inside wondered if Maceo had gotten all of his staff the way he'd hired her—by screwing them.

Cassie was watching her carefully. "*No* is the answer to the question you're not asking," she said with a wry grin. "I had a boyfriend when I met Maceo, one that I loved very much. So, no, Maceo and I didn't sleep together."

Ori was scarlet-faced. "I, um...."

"Ori, let's be real. Everyone knows you and Maceo are together. We're cool with it, so relax..." Cassie was grinning at her knowingly now, and Ori had to laugh.

Ori rolled over in bed and stretched. It had been two months since she'd returned to Italy and moved in with Maceo and it had been bliss. *Utter, complete heaven,* she thought now. Her body ached pleasantly from making love most of the night, and now, on this Saturday, she and Maceo had plans to do ... nothing. From the whirlwind of work, it was really the first time they had spent together that was free of work commitments and Ori was really looking forward to just hanging out with him.

They had become good friends as well as lovers, equal partners in their relationship despite Maceo's imposing wealth. Ori never felt at a disadvantage with him, even living in his opulent apartment.

She wondered where he'd gone now—maybe to fetch some breakfast. She got up and pulled her robe around her naked body. As she suspected, Maceo was in the kitchen, fighting with his new espresso machine and cursing loudly in Italian. He was bare-chested, just in his jeans, and she slid her arms around his waist.

"*Buongiorno*, beautiful ..." He bent his head to kiss her. She kissed him back and, in reply, opened her robe and pressed her bare skin against him. He groaned, and she giggled as he lifted her onto the countertop, pushing her legs apart and unzipping his jeans. "God, woman, you make me crazy."

He fucked her there, hard, until she was crying out his name in ecstasy and he was shooting hot, thick cum, deep inside her. Laughing and panting for air, they collapsed to the floor together.

"*Bella,* I love to fuck you, I really do," he said, puffing for air. "But God knows how we're going to get anything else done."

She wound her arms around his neck. "Today, my love, we don't have to."

And so, they lazed around the apartment, making love and talking, sending out for pizza when they got hungry.

The day went by too quickly for Ori's liking. Maceo grinned at her sulky face. "*Mio caro,* tomorrow is Sunday. We can do it all over again."

. . .

But a phone call changed everything in a heartbeat. At first, Ori frowned at the unknown cell phone number on her caller ID, but when she answered it the blood in her veins turned to ice and her legs gave way under her.

Maceo took the phone from her and talked to the person on the other end. By the time he ended the call, he knew that Ori's world had just collapsed and felt helpless to know how to fix it. Not even his money could help her now.

AJ was dead.

They told her it was a suicide but that they had not seen any signs of it. AJ had been doing well in his new program and had even talked about getting an apartment away from the facility with a friend he'd met there. Everything had seemed good and when Ori had talked to him he had been upbeat and positive.

Then, Friday afternoon, an orderly had found him on the concrete path outside the building. He had leaped from the roof. He was killed instantly, his brains smashed from his head by the impact.

A numb Ori let Maceo make all the arrangements for her, and they flew to California to claim his body and arrange the funeral.

But Tyson Janek had gotten there first, and now, with the tragic suicide of his son, he was a media darling again, all past mistakes forgiven. Ori sat through a media circus of a funeral, arranged by Tyson. It had been the exact opposite of what AJ would have wanted. Maceo kissed her gently. "Are you sure you'll be okay if I go out? I won't be long."

Ori nodded. They were in a hotel in San Francisco. Ori had not wanted to go back to Italy yet, wanting to be near AJ's grave a little while longer. Maceo had other plans. He was going to see Tyson Janek—not that he told Ori that. Tyson Janek was going to pay for what happened to AJ, and for what he'd done to Ori.

He walked into the restaurant where Tyson Janek was eating breakfast with a weasely-looking lackey. Maceo strode up to the table and glared at the aide. "Fuck off. Now."

The aide paled but looked at Tyson, who nodded. Maceo took the seat the aide vacated and stared at Janek.

Tyson sipped his coffee slowly, seemingly unfazed in the face of Maceo's overwhelming anger. "What do you want, Bartoli?"

Maceo gave him a chilly smile. "Only to tell you that once Ori is ready, we will be going to the authorities about the sustained and continued abuse she suffered at your hands."

Tyson shrugged. "And who is going to believe her? Where's the proof?"

Maceo's smile dropped, and his eyes took on a dangerous gleam. "I suppose you think the press, now that you're playing the grieving father card, will slam her for taking advantage at this time? They'll paint her a gold-digger? I think not. I have a feeling the press will soon be against you, Janek, and the scandal you've just weathered will seem like a walk in the park."

Tyson laughed loudly. "Really? And where are you getting this fairytale from?"

Maceo sat back, studying him carefully. "Because this world is fucked up, and because it blames the victim rather than the perpetrator, especially if the victim is female, you probably think, hey, who's going to believe her?"

Tyson inclined his head, and Maceo leaned forward. "Then how do you think the press will respond to a father raping his own son, Janek? You piece of utter shit. AJ told me everything."

To Maceo's satisfaction, Janek paled. "What the hell are you talking about?"

"You know damn well. You raped AJ, just like you did Ori. You're a monster and, believe me, I'm going to make sure the world knows it."

MACEO GOT up and stalked out of the restaurant. Tyson stared after him, then plucked his cell phone out of his pocket. "It's me. He's just left. Do it now." Ori had just gotten dressed when Maceo called her. "I'm on my way back now, *bella*. I'll see you soon."

Ori smiled. "Good. I missed you." She scooped her long dark hair into a messy ponytail and grabbed her book from the nightstand, intending to read until Maceo got back.

As she walked back into the main suite, a movement caught her eye. She turned, and he was on her. A masked figure, twice her size, threw her to the ground. Ori, her mind panicked and confused, had no time to fight back as the attacker brandished a knife.

Oh god. No, please ...

Ori had no time to scream ...

If you want to continue reading this story, you can get your copy from your favorite vendor by searching for the title:

The Midnight Club

You can also find the e-book version by typing this link in your computer's browser:

https://www.hotandsteamyromance.com/products/the-midnight-club

OTHER BOOKS BY THIS AUTHOR

Saving Her Rescuer: A Billionaire & A Virgin Romance

I was just trying to get away from my crazy ex for the weekend when I ended up in a giant pileup on the highway up to Gore Mountain.

https://geni.us/SavingHerRescuer

～

Sensual Sounds: A Rockstar Ménage

Lust. Lies. Double lives.

The rock and roll industry is full of people who are looking out for themselves and willing to do anything to rise to the top.

https://www.hotandsteamyromance.com/collections/frontpage/products/sensual-sounds-a-rockstar-menage

～

On the Run: A Secret Baby Romance

Murder. Lies. Fraud. Just another day in the lives of billionaires and women on the run.

https://www.hotandsteamyromance.com/collections/frontpage/products/on-the-run-a-secret-baby-romance

The Dirty Doctor's Touch: A Billionaire Doctor Romance

I am a master. An elitist. I am at the top of my field, and I know what I am doing.

https://www.hotandsteamyromance.com/collections/frontpage/products/the-dirty-doctor-s-touch-a-billionaire-doctor-romance

∽

The Hero She Needs: A Single Daddy Next Door Romance

He's the only man I've ever wanted...

https://www.hotandsteamyromance.com/collections/frontpage/products/the-hero-she-needs-a-single-daddy-next-door-romance

∽

You can find all of my books here:

Hot and Steamy Romance

https://www.hotandsteamyromance.com

ABOUT THE AUTHOR

Mrs. Love writes about smart, sexy women and the hot alpha billionaires who love them. She has found her own happily ever after with her dream husband and adorable 6 and 2 year old kids.

Currently, Michelle is hard at work on the next book in the series, and trying to stay off the Internet.

"Thank you for supporting an indie author. Anything you can do, whether it be writing a review, or even simply telling a fellow reader that you enjoyed this. Thanks

Facebook
facebook.com/HotAndSteamyRomance

Instagram
instagram.com/michellesromance

©Copyright 2020 by Michelle Love - All rights Reserved

In no way is it legal to reproduce, duplicate, or transmit any part of this document in either electronic means or in printed format. Recording of this publication is strictly prohibited and any storage of this document is not allowed unless with written permission from the publisher. All rights are reserved.

Respective authors own all copyrights not held by the publisher.

www.ingramcontent.com/pod-product-compliance
Lightning Source LLC
LaVergne TN
LVHW021702060526
838200LV00050B/2470